ARMOR

THE FIGHT FOR SICILY

A NOVEL OF WW2 TANK WARFARE
CRAIG DiLOUIE

Editing by Timothy Johnson. Cover art by
Eloise Knapp Design.

Published by ZING Communications, Inc.

www.CraigDiLouie.com

HISTORICAL NOTE

While this book is based on real events occurring during Operation Husky in Sicily in 1943, significant artistic license was taken to create a compelling work of fiction. The most significant example of this is Destroyer Company fighting at both Gela and then shifting to Licata in a compressed timeline. Otherwise, every effort was taken to capture what it was like to be in a tank crew participating in the invasion of Sicily in July 1943. Any errors, of course, are the author's. If you're a history buff and see any errors you'd like to share with the author, email him at Read@CraigDiLouie.com.

"When we land, we will meet German and Italian soldiers whom it is our honor and privilege to attack and destroy... God is with us. We will win."

—General George S. Patton's address to Seventh Army before the Sicily landings

THE STAGE:

OPERATION HUSKY

Despite the humiliating Allied defeat at Kasserine Pass in February 1943, the Tunisian campaign yielded a spectacular victory by May with the surrender of all Axis forces. The Allies had finally secured North Africa.

While still far from Berlin, the Allied forces had achieved significant results. The campaign made the Mediterranean safer for Allied shipping, eliminated the Axis threat to Middle Eastern oilfields, and shortened convoy routes with Britain's reopening of the Suez Canal.

As the Tunisian campaign drew to a close, Allied leaders faced the question: Where to next?

They'd already drawn up plans to invade Sicily. By taking the ten-thousand-square-mile Italian island, the Allies hoped to complete their domination of the Mediterranean while possibly enticing Italy to break its alliance with Germany.

In July 1943, 160,000 Allied troops boarded a vast armada at ports across North Africa. Led by General George S. Patton and General Bernard Montgomery, these forces prepared for another hard fight.

Toughened by Tunisia, the Americans were ready to invade Europe.

MOROCCO

CHAPTER ONE

WAR GAMES

Barracks bags slung over shoulders, the four tankers hopped off the deuce-and-a-half and scanned the chaotic tent city and tank park. Ten thousand strong, 2nd Armored Division consisted of tank, infantry, and field artillery battalions plus signal, recon, tank recovery, maintenance, and supply units.

Corporal Anthony Russo was glad to be back among his own. While waiting for transport in Casablanca, he and his comrades had decided to see the sights. A wrong turn took them into the Arab Quarter, a maze of twisting, crowded alleys where people lived in abject poverty. Here, Americans had been killed just for their clothes. A crowd of beggars formed followed by some toughs, and the tankers were lucky to escape unharmed.

Russo had been harmed enough already. They all had—him in his legs, Swanson across his chest, Wade along his back, Ackley in his shin, Clay just about everywhere you can be hurt.

While Clay remained in an Algiers hospital, the other tankers' rehabilitation had been cut short with orders to ship out to Morocco. One didn't have to listen to the latrine rumors to know something big was going to happen.

Swanson snatched Russo's kit bag and swung it over his other massive shoulder. "I'll take that for you, Mac.

You walk like you haven't taken a shit in a week."

"You're half right," Russo said.

"Where's the lieutenant?" Ackley said, his tone revealing he didn't really care where the lieutenant was but wanted to change the subject.

"Here comes the Professor," the loader said. "He knows everything."

Swanson no longer called the gunner *Wisenheimer* but instead *Professor*, which still sounded derogatory but marked a slight improvement in their relations. Russo was still *Mac*, though it was said with less derision.

Wade returned from asking around, grimacing from his still-aching wounds. "We found our regiment. D Company isn't far."

Russo plodded in tow. After being rousted in the middle of the night and packed onto a truck for the long, bumpy drive to the camp, he was ready for a hot and a cot. It was barely dawn, and the tankers were already up and at 'em as the African sun just started to bleach the eastern horizon.

But he was smiling. It was good to be back.

The men found their platoon commander and saluted. Lieutenant Pierce was gaunt and prematurely balding, his sharp face slightly softened by gleaming round spectacles and an easy smile. He appeared more like a gentleman farmer than a tank commander, but that was the Army. Most of the American fighting men still didn't feel like real soldiers, and only a few of them, like the hard-bitten Sergeant Garrett, looked the part.

The lieutenant returned their salute and held out his hand to shake. The tankers introduced themselves. Corporal Russo, Sergeant Wade, Corporal Swanson. General Patton had honored his promise to promote them all.

Pierce scrutinized Ackley. "And who's this?"

The kid wrinkled his nose. "I'm Ackley."

"He's our driver," Russo said. "One of the only survivors of a whole other massacre."

"Welcome to Destroyer Company, the Hell on Wheels," the lieutenant said. "We'll get you billeted, but first let me show you around."

He pointed out the dining facility, showers, water tankers, latrines, PX, maintenance collection area called the *boneyard*, and medical tents. Then he gestured to a cluster of armored vehicles. "This is us. Your tank's here too. We just got it a few days ago, fresh off the boat."

The M4 medium tanks were Duck Soup, Dealer, Democracy, and the lieutenant's own Delilah. Their crews paused from doing maintenance work on the big vehicles to check out the newcomers.

When Pierce got to the last tank, his face darkened. "Looks like somebody named it for you."

In big white letters, *DOG* was emblazoned on the turret over the fresh green paint job.

"Golly," Ackley said. "I surely hope that ain't an omen."

Some of the tankers snickered. Somebody barked.

"Paint whatever you want over it," the lieutenant said. "A crew should be allowed to name their own home."

"I kind of like it," Wade said.

"They could have named it Dildo for all I care," Swanson said. "If it moves and shoots and has a coupla inches of armor, I'm good."

"We'll take it as is," confirmed Russo, who considered it a point of pride to always turn a practical joke around by making it seem like a surprise gift.

Pierce wasn't listening. His face darkened again. "And who put a goddamn Confederate flag on my Delilah?" The snickers started again. "I'd better see Old Glory flying again before we go back out, you chumps."

"Our last commander had a Texas flag on his," Russo said.

"Yeah? What happened to him?"

"He rammed a Tiger tank and shot its commander out of the cupola."

Pierce smiled and shook his head. "That's a Texan, all right."

"Then he got blown up."

The smile evaporated. "Well, you guys have been in it, so I don't have to tell you what's what. Maybe whatever luck you got from that charm up your ass will rub off on my jokers. We'll be seeing action soon."

After a relatively easy invasion during Operation Torch, 2nd Armored had sat on its heels during the Tunisian campaign. While elements entered Tunisia and fought after Kasserine, the bulk had stayed here in Casablanca, tasked with deterring fascist Spain from crossing into Africa while training for a fight that hadn't yet come.

"Do we have a bog, sir?"

"Go to the repple-depple, they'll get you sorted."
The replacement depot. "First, I want you to get your
gear stowed and grab some chow. Then get your big
boy ready to roll out. The company is going out for our
second training exercise of the day. You might as well
join in."

Wade blinked. "Your second time out?"

"We've been at it since 0400," Pierce explained.
"This is Morocco in June, guys. We get our training
done early. Gets real hot in a tank at midday. I'm talking
a hundred forty degrees hot."

Russo had experienced that on the train, crammed
into a sweltering sleeper car with rowdy infantrymen
who opened all the windows to let in some air only to
choke the car with grimy black coal smoke from the
engine stack.

"We'll be glad for the practice," he said, though he
didn't appreciate having to do any training after being
up half the night. "We're pretty rusty."

"We practiced an amphibious invasion last week.
Rolled onto one of those new landing crafts the Navy
cooked up, sailed around, rolled back off. Today, we're
shooting targets in the bush, just like we used to at Fort
Knox."

"We'll get right to it," Russo said.

The tankers stowed their bags, wolfed down a quick
breakfast, and returned to the tank. As tired as they
were, they all were eager to take Dog for a walk.

For months, they'd convalesced at the hospital
in Algiers until they'd recovered enough to begin

rehabilitation. Though they could have used more rest before returning to combat, they were eager to escape from pushing brooms and censoring mail and get back into an M4's fighting compartment.

"Ack-Ack, help me get the engine bay open," Swanson said, smiling.

Russo was polishing a periscope lens. "What are you so happy about?"

"Dog's got a loader's hatch. When we get hit, I'll be out in two shakes of a lamb's tail."

"I think you mean, *if*."

"Whatever you say, Mac."

While they checked the track tension, fluids, and filter, a grinning tanker sauntered over. "You fellas get your African campaign badges?"

Russo finished his polishing. "Yup."

"Even though you weren't here." The tanker called out to his friends, "See what I was telling you? They're giving the campaign badge to the replacements!"

"Because they aren't replacements, you imbecile," his sergeant said. "They're Old Ironsides. They fought in Tunisia, which is more than I can say for you."

While his crewmates laughed at him, the tanker stomped his feet and did an awkward bow that ended in a grimace. "Aw, jeez. Sorry, fellas."

"Glad we got the ass-sniffing out of the way," Swanson said and returned to sink his arms into Dog's engine bay.

Chuckling, the tank sergeant strolled over and singled out Wade for his stripes. "Don't mind him, Sergeant. He ain't right in the head on account that big chip on his shoulder keeps smacking into it."

Russo offered his hand. "Good to meet you. I command Dog."

While they shook, the man glanced at Wade, who said, "It's how we do it."

"Hey, whatever works. Sorry about that, Corporal."

"Call me Tony."

The tank sergeant's homely, sunburned face stretched into a smile. "Tony it is. I'm Mickey. Mickey Cranston. Duck Soup's my gal." He pointed. "Butch commands Dealer, and Butter over there has Democracy."

Russo looked them over and saw average joes like him, men who'd come for the adventure and stayed because they had no choice.

"Butter?" Wade said. "Sounds like there's a story there."

"Not really. He collects butterflies." The tank sergeant lit a short cigar and tossed the match. "You hear anything where you came from? About where we're going?"

"Probably the same as you," Russo said. "Just latrine rumors."

"I doubt we're going to England and invading France," Wade cut in.

Mickey exhaled a cloud of blue smoke. "Why do you say that?"

The gunner shrugged. "We're all here. It's easier to invade someplace close than ship us all the way back to the UK. My guess is Sardinia."

"Why Sardinia?"

"Sicily's the obvious choice, but the Germans are expecting us to do that. Sardinia's the other obvious choice."

Mickey laughed. "So no France, I can buy that. A guy in signals said he heard it from a source he trusts we're going to the Balkans."

Wade thought it over. "I doubt even our brass is that dumb. We'll probably invade Sardinia and then Italy."

"Why Italy?"

"Because we'll all be in Sardinia."

Mickey laughed again. "You've got a good grasp of military strategy, pal. You ought to be a general."

"This is Hawkeye," Russo said. "He's our deep thinker."

"Yeah, I got one of those too. Mine's a bit of a pain in the ass, though."

Swanson guffawed from the engine bay.

Waving his index finger, Pierce marched among the tanks. "Let's move out, Destroyers! Crank up your big boys and start your engines!"

Russo hauled himself onto the sponson and paused to massage his stiff leg. Then he lowered himself into the cupola, plugged in, and grinned. The comms check confirmed the radio and interphone were operational.

He puffed out his chest in pride. "Driver, start the engine!"

Ackley worked the controls. The tank's four-hundred-horsepower engine roared to life and revved. "Everything checks out, Mac."

"Fantastic." Russo patted the hull. "Good Dog." The

American Locomotive Company had built her well. "*Mannaggia dial!*" *I curse the devil!*

"We'll be in the lead, so look smart," the lieutenant said over the radio.

In an orderly column two vehicles abreast, the Destroyers rumbled out of the camp onto a wide dirt road. A support train of jeeps, tank recovery vehicles, ambulances, and deuce-and-a-half trucks rolled after them.

Past the checkpoint with its crude guardhouse, the road snaked southeast through farmland into hill country, which was already shimmering in the morning heat. Beyond, the brown humps and cones of the Middle Atlas lay heaped under an azure sky.

Too preoccupied with scratching a living to pay attention to the column, barley farmers leaned against oxen-drawn ploughs. The scene reminded Russo how, at Sidi bou Zid, the farmers had kept at it even with shells shrieking over their heads. It gave him the odd feeling of being in a stranger's house. He found it a little embarrassing how people just went on trying to live their lives while he rolled around their neighborhood, playing war games with real ammunition.

"Now every young *tanker*, who was in Casa*blanca*," Mickey sang in a surprisingly clear, strong tenor.

The platoon frequency filled with laughter and ribald comments.

"Knows Stella, the Belle of Fe*dala*..."

The other commanders joined in, "*A can of C ration will whip up a passion, in this little gal of Fedala!*"

Russo sighed with longing, imagining what this

legendary French lady looked like and wishing he could meet her himself. Then he sighed again, this time from fulfillment. He was back in a tank, officially its commander. Plus he was an E-4 now, which paid $66 a month, most of which he sent home to his proud parents in Trenton, New Jersey. The war could give as well as take, though it took far more than it gave and always threatened to take it all.

The column stopped in a fallow field at the base of a low hill. Pierce explained the regiment had set up a course over the rise. Wood targets representing machine gun nests, infantry, tanks, and antitank guns had to be identified and destroyed.

"Captain says we're starting now," Pierce buzzed over the radio. "Button up and form a line on my three."

"We're the end of the line, Ackley," Russo said. "Watch out for that big rock. Wait until we're past it—"

"I know," Ackley said, all irritation.

"Now advance and give 'em hell," the lieutenant said.

"For Stella!" Butch yelled from Dealer's cupola.

The M4 tanks lurched over the rise with a roar. The commanders called out targets. Whoever had developed the course had given them a doozy designed to test the tankers' ability to fight together. A machine gun nest menaced the platoon from fifty yards on their right flank, while a tank and two antitank guns stood on the opposite hill in defiladed positions.

Pierce dissected the problem in an instant and belted out orders. Aside from a copse of palm trees partway down the hill, there was no concealment, though concealment didn't matter right now, only cover did. Unfortunately, the only option for cover was to back up and take a hull-down position.

Reversing, Duck Soup dropped white phosphorous in front of one of the antitank guns to blind it until it could be dealt with later, then joined Democracy in firing high-explosive rounds at the other gun.

"One, Two, Five, knock out that tank!" the radio blared.

In the platoon, Dog was Five.

"Gunner, tank, shot, five hundred, fire!" Russo yelled.

"On the way!" Dog bucked at the recoil.

The shell streaked across the gully and blazed a trench into the hillside. Russo winced as if it had ripped a hole in his gut. He heard the din of battle as *panzers* rumbled toward him in a haze of gun smoke and exhaust. He wished they would stop but was terrified when they did because that was when they fired—

He snapped out of it. "Driver, right stick and take us along the rise so we're in front of that MG crew. Gunner, up four, right four. Traverse as we turn. *Mannaggia dial!*"

"American, Mac!" Swanson said. "Up!"

"On the way!"

Another miss. Delilah claimed the kill, her shell smashing the target. Dirt fountained into the air and left a crater.

Feeling sick now, Russo started to give the order to shift targets, but HE rounds ranged the exposed antitank gun and pulverized it. Which was all well and good, this being a team effort and the goal being survival under fire.

That left the machine gun nest.

"Driver, left stick, high gear, advance. Run those *disgraziats* down!"

Wade was already shooting with the coax machine gun. While the rest of the platoon raced whooping down the hill to take out the next antitank gun still shrouded in smoke, Dog rolled on top of the enemy MG position and flattened it. Ackley jerked the tank in a shimmy to grind it into splinters.

A black cloud poured over the opposite hill.

Russo raised his binoculars and yelled into the radio, "Sandstorm!"

He actually wasn't sure what the hell it was, but it was big and dark and growing. It'd be on him in seconds. He dropped into the turret and pulled the hatch closed after him as the cloud closed in.

"What the hell?" Swanson said at his scope. "They're bugs!"

"Locusts," Wade clarified. "Amazing."

The swarm swept over the tank with a skin-crawling shimmering sound from the flapping of millions of wings. Their bodies pattered against the hull. The tankers sweated in oven heat as the rising African sun slowly cooked the tank.

"Just like Tunisia," the loader growled. "Everything is trying to kill us."

"They came as far as Algeria," the gunner went on in a lecturing drone. "It's been hotter and drier than usual, which makes them swarm. A single swarm can cover a hundred square miles."

"Stop talking," Swanson said.

Russo raised his scope to see for himself. Thousands of grayish-yellow, spotted locusts flitted past. Then one landed on the scope, followed by more until it was covered in a seething carpet of bugs.

He asked, "Can anybody see?"

"I can't see shit," the loader fumed. "It's like that calamity that happened to the pharaoh—"

"The eighth plague of Egypt," Wade said.

"Exactly what was I going to say, Professor. It's like we share the same mind."

The gunner shuddered. "Ugh." Whether to the bugs or the idea or sharing the loader's mind, Russo didn't know.

Irritated voices filled the radio.

"Looks like everybody's blind," he said.

In more ways than one. During the exercise, the other tank commanders had congratulated each other on their fine shooting, having fun with it. Russo knew it was a whole different experience while under direct panzer fire.

The truth was the Germans would have attacked first, and in tank combat, whoever shot first had a big advantage. Their initial salvos would likely have left one or more of the platoon's tanks a burning wreck.

"We'd better get moving," Ackley said. "We stay here much longer, we're gonna melt in this heat."

Orders came through to drive through the swarm and return to base. Russo lowered his goggles and raised his handkerchief to cover his eyes and face.

So far, this whole damn war is the blind leading the blind, he thought.

Russo hoped, wherever they were sent next, command wouldn't revisit the same mistakes that had plagued the army in Tunisia. He hoped whoever was in charge, Patton or anybody else, had gained enough experience they could see clearly and prevent another disaster.

Then he raised the hatch. Instantly, the tank filled with flying insects, which set the tankers to cursing as Dog stumbled back to camp.

CHAPTER TWO

REPPLE-DEPPLE

Private First Class Leonard Payne was fighting fascism by peeling potatoes.

A hundred-pound sack of potatoes, to be exact.

Seven months ago, he had sold several paintings at his first gallery show in Greenwich Village, New York City. He'd finally made it as an artist. At the after party, his friends smoked a lot of cigarettes and drank a lot of cheap wine. They talked about the war, as they often did, and agreed the best way to fight fascism was to inspire with art that celebrated freedom of the human spirit.

It was all grand stuff, but Payne had enough of it. His heroes were the tough leftists who went to Spain to fight fascists during the Spanish Civil War. Men of action. While war was evil, he thought some wars were worth picking up a rifle, and this was one of them. He didn't want to inspire others to resist anymore. It was time for him to step up and put his body on the line for his beliefs.

After selling his first paintings, he found himself with extra cash in his pocket and a burgeoning reputation in the art world. He'd done something big for himself, and now it was time to put others first. In his mind, this was the perfect time to enlist. The Army sent him to Armored Force School.

He'd arrived in Morocco with orders to report to a replacement battalion, where he'd spent the majority of his time doing a whole lot of nothing because there had been very few casualties to replace. Three months now, and he hadn't fired a shot, not once since his training at Fort Knox.

Mess Sergeant Buster Jackson emerged from the mess tent wearing an apron splattered with tomato sauce. "How are you making out here?"

"All right, I guess."

The Black chief cook ran a quick count on the remaining potatoes. "Yup, you're doing fine. Stick with me, son. It's the best job in the army."

"It's not as bad as I thought it would be," Payne admitted. Fact was, he enjoyed creation far more than destruction, even if he was only creating dinner. "I'd rather be in a front-line unit, though. Doing my part."

He'd volunteered for kitchen police duty because there wasn't much else to do at the replacement center other than guard duty and training, all of it tedious busywork. After he figured out the repple-depple master sergeant didn't do roll call before the day's training, he started skipping it.

He'd gotten a pass and checked out the sights in Casablanca with the Brownie camera he'd picked up for two dollars on his way to the war. The squalor piled against the opulent French Quarter cured him of any interest in seeing the sights. More than ever, he missed New York and its bustle, especially the smell and chatter of women. Most of all, he missed painting. He longed to work, but he didn't think art had a place in war.

With nothing to do other than periodic guard duty shifts, he'd started eyeing kitchen police duty. Back at Armored Force School, KP was punishment for any infraction ranging from a lackluster boot shine to wearing a shit-eating grin. Volunteering for KP duty meant getting up extra early and working into the evening, but Payne didn't mind. He'd worked hard jobs in factories, stores, and the docks. KP would give him something to do that was actually useful. It offered fleeting hours of excitement-catatonia similar to what he experienced when he was painting. Like painting, manual labor was good for the soul.

"The war effort needs guys like us as much as it needs guys in the tanks," Jackson told him. "Plus you eat all you want, and everybody treats you nice."

The soldiers knew, if they buttered up the kitchen staff, their next plate might have a little extra hot food on it. Bully them, and you got less.

"You haven't heard them complain about shit on a shingle," Payne said.

The first order of the day was to fire the big coffee pots, followed by preparing a hot breakfast. The meal sometimes included toast with creamed ground beef on it, which the troops called *SOS*, or *shit on a shingle*.

"I hear them," Jackson said. "I also see them eat it. Soldiers got to bitch about something. Army food ain't bad. There's only bad cooks."

"You're a good cook," Payne said.

"I can swing it so you stay on with me. Get you a technician grade." The mess sergeant inspected him.

"You'd rather be off fighting, though. I can read it on your stupid face. Cooking ain't exciting enough for you."

Payne figured this was a break, so he wiped his hands on a rag and lit a cigarette. "I want to be useful. If that means scrubbing pots, I'm good with it. But at some point, I have to put myself on the line like the other guys."

"Fair enough. I'll take you as long as I can anyway. You don't bitch and you don't get in everybody's way and you're careful with the knives and you don't sneak more than your fair share of extra ice cream."

As Jackson went back into the tent, Payne ground out his cigarette, policed it, and went back to peeling against fascism.

Every day, all their hard work led to the big event: dinner. Soldiers tramped into the dining facility, grabbed trays—which they'd dubbed *garbage catchers*—and lined up for their chow.

In the steam rising from the big metal vats, Payne sweat as he served out spaghetti and sauce. Whatever the men thought of Army food in general, they loved spaghetti and, for a change of pace, restricted their bitching to the subjects of officers and the weather. Another man relieved him so he could bus tables.

"Patton is all sizzle and no steak," he overheard an artillery corporal telling his comrades at a table.

Payne caught all his latrine talk from random conversation snatches in the mess. The men often talked about George S. Patton, the commanding general.

"Twenty-five-dollar fine for any man he catches not wearing a helmet and tie? He can stay in Tunisia long as he wants."

"I don't know," said a private. "I think he's got dash. I heard he learned to fly a plane to learn about air attacks. Sailed a boat to Hawaii to learn about sea travel. He designed a cavalry sword for the Army."

"Which his cavalrymen used when he ordered them to clear the Bonus Army out of Washington," another man growled. "Against his fellow Great War veterans asking for early redemption of their war bonus certificates."

"That was MacArthur. Patton was just following orders. He's got more balls than all the rest put together. We need a guy like that."

"We're part of his fate, and he's fated for glory," the corporal said. "Our blood's just grease for the wheels."

Payne heaved his tub full of greasy plates to the next table, where a tanker stood leaning on the table watching the repple-depple master sergeant eat.

"I'm not bothering the lieutenant right now," the master sergeant said. "You can fill out the requisition forms tomorrow and wait."

The other man jerked his thumb at Payne. "How about this guy?"

The master sergeant shrugged. "How about him?"

The man squinted as he appraised Payne in his skivvy shirt and dirty apron. "I'm Sergeant Charles Wade. What's your name, soldier?"

"Private First Class Leonard Payne."

"You assigned to this, or are you a replacement?"

"I'm a replacement. I went to Armored Force School."

"What training did you get?"

"I got in about twenty-five hours driving an M4. Fired the gun a few times."

"What'd you do back home?"

"A little of this, a little of that."

"You're a man of few words," Wade said. "You're hired."

"Come back tomorrow, do the paperwork, and you got him," the master sergeant said. "Now shove off, and let me finish my supper in peace."

"Be ready at 0900," Wade told Payne.

And just like that, he became a tanker.

Buster Jackson took the news in stride. "That's how the cookie crumbles. Good luck to you."

Payne shook his hand. "Thanks, Buster. I'll miss the extra dessert."

"Speaking of which, hang on a minute." The man disappeared and returned with a handful of Oh Henry! bars. "Take these, and hide them for a rainy day."

"Thank you. This is great."

"Now finish mopping the floor, so we can get out of here."

The next morning, Payne helped serve breakfast and reported on time with his barracks bag to the master sergeant, who handed him over to Sergeant Wade. Wade led him through the bustling camp toward his new home, which was Second Platoon, Company D.

Along the way, the tank sergeant shot him looks as if he was dying to ask something.

"Whatever's on your mind," Payne said, "you can ask me."

"Did you bring any books with you?"

He chuckled. "Lots. *The Great Gatsby, Frankenstein,* some Shakespeare—"

"Leonard, you just made a friend."

"What do you have?"

"Very little. I've been paying top dollar for every book I can find, but most of the guys around here, their idea of a classic read is Captain America. My own library got burned up when we lost Boomer at Sidi bou Zid."

"You were in Tunisia?"

"The whole crew was. Don't expect any glamorous stories, though. We don't really talk about it."

Payne shrugged. "I'm just happy I'm with a veteran crew that knows what it's doing."

"You'll be on the bow gun, where you can watch and learn. Just do your job, ignore everything else, and the Germans will take care of the rest."

They weaved between rolling jeeps and hustling soldiers in the busy tank park and stopped at a tank with *DOG* painted on the turret. The giant green vehicles were nothing to look at, even ugly from an aesthetic perspective, but Payne couldn't help but be impressed. They were modern knights, lance and warrior and squires and warhorse all packed into a single tracked machine.

Judging composition and light, Payne pulled his

Brownie camera from his kit and looped the strap around his neck.

A big, hairy tanker grinned down at him from the 75 barrel. "Lookie what the cat dragged in, green as grass."

"This is Leonard Payne," Wade said to the crew. "Our new bog." He pointed and called out the names of the men Payne would be living and fighting alongside for the duration.

"Did you bring the Professor any good books?"

Payne glanced at Wade, who said, "He means me."

Swanson went on, "The Prof don't like girlie mags. You see him get in the shitter ahead of you with *Ulysses*, you'll just have to hold it."

The tankers laughed. Payne joined in.

The man glared down at him. "What are you laughing at, Cherry?"

"What you said was funny. I get lost in a good book on the can too."

"Don't I know you from someplace?"

"I worked in the D-fac."

"If only we needed a guy who could scrub pots and pans, Payne in my ass."

Payne reached into his bag and produced the Oh Henry! bars. "All that KP duty did get me these, if you guys want one."

Jackson had told him to save them for a rainy day, but he didn't believe in rainy days. He'd lived hand to mouth for so long he believed only in what today offered.

"Why didn't you say so?" Swanson jumped off the

sponson and snatched one. "We got off on the wrong foot, looks like." He tore his bar's wrapper and took a massive bite. "Now if you want to be really useful," he paused to munch, "get your ass to the motor pool, and don't come back without a fallopian tube."

Russo nodded sagely. "Make that two, *goombah*. That way we'll have a spare."

"Ask for Sergeant Colbert personally. He'll get you squared away."

Ackley joined in. "You find a can of squelch while you're there, bring me one. I'm fresh out."

"Sure," Payne said.

He stowed his bag on the tank and found Wade on the other side, sitting with his back against the tracks. Candy bar in one hand and *Henry V* in the other, the tank sergeant looked like the happiest man in the world. Payne stared at him, translating the scene to canvas in his mind. He opened his Brownie's shutter and snapped a picture.

The gunner read aloud, "*When I bestride him, I soar, I am a hawk: he trots the air; the earth sings when he touches it; the basest horn of his hoof is more musical than the pipe of Hermes.* I wonder what Shakespeare would make of tanks." He looked up. "You getting settled in?"

"Corporal Swanson wants me to get him a fallopian tube."

"Of course he does."

"I was just wondering why he wants a piece of female anatomy."

Wade snickered. "It's a snipe hunt, a hazing ritual.

High comedy for him."

"I figure the same goes for a can of squelch, whatever that is."

"Just go and play the fool and get it over with."

Payne shrugged. "Sure."

He walked off into the camp. The day was heating up and promised to be another scorcher. At last, he came across a supply depot and found what he was looking for.

He returned to the tank and discovered the men had gone off somewhere, leaving him alone to carry out his project. Dog really was ugly but again also strangely compelling. The crew had tied cut logs to its side armor, a primitive adornment to a modern monster. Handholds, perhaps? He noticed the rest of the platoon had the same timber strapped to their hulls. An aesthetic statement? He took another picture on his Kodak film.

Time to make his own contribution. He climbed onto the rear deck, which was piled with supplies and gear, and set the paintbrushes and paints he'd scored at the supply depot. White, green, red, and blue. Believing Payne wanted them for the mess and hoping to ingratiate himself, the supply sergeant had handed them over with minimal hassle.

"*Wear me as a seal over your heart, as a seal upon your arm, for love is strong as death, passion cruel as the grave,*" he quoted aloud as he got to work.

Payne cleaned the turret surface, sketched out his idea with a pencil, and started brushing with his acrylic paints. Time dilated as his brain reached a kind of fugue state. It was similar to what he'd experienced working in the frantic D-fac, but with painting, he had something beautiful at the end, something he'd created.

He smiled while he scratched a deep, nagging itch that he hadn't even known he'd had. When he finished, paint was splattered on his uniform like a bad attempt at camouflage. He lit a cigarette while he waited for his work to dry.

After his smoke, he climbed into the turret and sat in the commander's station. Corporal "Shorty" Russo would stand up here, his eyes eleven feet above the ground. Next, Payne sat at the other stations to see what the crew would see, so he could empathize with them while they were rolling.

The turret had turned hot as an oven. The stench of sweat and ass overpowered the headache-inducing fumes of the factory paint job. At last, he sat in his own seat behind the .30-cal machine gun. He wrapped his hand around the grip and imagined firing it, men toppling under a withering stream of bullets. The vision made him recoil in disgust back out into the open air, where it was a little cooler.

The rest of the crew returned looking glum. Other tankers were coming back as well, shouting with excitement and with their index fingers in the air.

"We're number one?" Payne guessed.

"It's an *I* for invasion, goofus," Swanson growled. "We're shipping out. Did you get the fallopian..."

The loader stopped. The crew all stared at his painting.

Payne gazed upon it like he was seeing it for the

first time. He'd reworked the crudely scrawled *DOG* to stylize the lettering into strong capitals. Beside it, he'd depicted a tough junkyard bulldog wearing a tanker's helmet and smoking a fat cigar.

"Wow," Ackley said. "Look at that." The kid, whom Payne had guessed was the unflappable type, was actually impressed.

"Yeah." Wade grinned. "That's something."

Russo shot him a glance. "Is it allowed?"

"It is now," Swanson said. "Because that there dog is me to a tee."

"Looks like our Dog's a he, not a she," Ackley said.

"Nice going, Payne," Wade said. "You just gave ol' Dog a personality."

Seeing the effect his art had on the men made Payne smile, and he thought, *Maybe art does have a place in war. Maybe war is the perfect place for it.*

CHAPTER THREE

ARMADA

After eight days in Morocco, the tankers along with the rest of their regiment boarded a train headed back to Oran. A big operation was in the works, but all they knew was they were going back to the war.

It turned out only a hundred flatcars in all of North Africa could carry a thirty-ton M4, and the French colonial railway system was a teetering mess even before ten thousand men clamored for passage with all their heavy equipment.

The train clacked along the tracks at a sluggish pace. Wondering if they'd ever get there, Tank Sergeant Charles Wade stared out the window at rows of almond trees. The purple Atlas Mountains and blue sky sprawled beyond. The other tankers in his crew played poker for cigarettes, but Wade didn't want to play cards. Although he could read the probabilities better than the other men, Swanson knew all his tells and cleaned him out every time.

Instead, he cracked open *The Great Gatsby*. Men shouted across the overcrowded sleeper car, and the stale air reeked of sweat, but he didn't care if they ever made it to Oran. He had plenty of books and time to read them. For him, this was as close to heaven as the Army could provide.

Within a few hours, the African sun turned the car into a rumbling oven. Wade wiped his forehead with his sleeve and tried to focus, but sweat was pouring off him now. He was melting.

His crew had endured this hell during the long journey to Morocco and knew what to expect, but the other tankers grumbled.

Wade stood and raised his hands. "Listen, guys. Whatever you do, don't open the windows. You'll regret it."

"Game is five card draw." Russo dealt another round of cards and glanced at Wade. "You know they're not going to listen—"

A tank crew opened several windows and stuck their heads out like dogs grinning from the window of the family car on a Sunday drive. Thick, choking smoke from the train stack rushed into the car and set all the men to hacking.

Swanson waved at the air with his cards. "You were born to command, Professor. A real leader of men."

Wade slouched back into his seat. "You cured me of that notion long ago."

"Close the windows, you goddamn morons," Captain Ratliff, Destroyer Company's commander, yelled.

The men snapped to it, coughing as black grime settled on everything.

"See? That's how you command. Do what I say or taste my boot." The loader inspected his cards and put two down. "I'll take two."

The captain was as big as Swanson but without an

ounce of fat on him. His arms seemed carved of rock. He smoked cigars and called the Germans *Heinies*.

"I'm not him." Wade found the captain naturally intimidating.

Russo nudged him. "You make a bet in the company pool?"

"Yeah."

"What'd you pick?"

"Sardinia. It's a safe bet. What about you?"

"Same." Russo next nudged Payne, who was staring through his camera lens at the almond trees with the strap looped around his neck. "What about you, New Guy?"

"I have no idea, so I didn't bet. I'll find out when I get there. In the end, it doesn't really matter."

"Way to take all the fun out of it," Swanson said. "And it's your turn."

Payne glanced at his cards and said, "I'm good with what I have."

"When are you gonna take my picture?"

"When you're nice to somebody. In case somebody wants to see proof."

The men laughed, and even Swanson smirked.

Wade liked their new bog; hell, all of them did. The man had an affinity for painting and taking pictures, and he had a taste for good literature, but otherwise, Wade didn't really know much about him. Mostly, he liked Payne because he had an aura of confidence like he'd been around the block a few times. His name begged for a variety of rich nicknames, but so far, there'd been no takers, and they'd settled on calling him

New Guy or, more often than not, just *bog*.

"Don't ask me, cuz I ain't telling," Ackley said.

"Nobody was, Ack-Ack," Swanson said.

"Then you won't know where we're going, but I've got a sure thing."

"That just leaves you, Mad Dog," Russo said. "Where do you think they're sending us?"

The loader flashed an evil grin. "That's my little secret, *Duce*."

Swanson still called Russo *Mac* for *Macaroni* but, for kicks, also started calling him *Il Duce* after Mussolini's title, which meant *The Leader*. He'd explained this suited Shorty's new role as tank commander. As always, the loader preferred to play with his victims, twisting the knife over months rather than killing them outright.

Russo wasn't impressed. "It's pronounced *Doo-chay*, not *Doo-chee*."

"Like I said. *Doo-chee*."

"Speaking of nicknames," Ackley said, "every time you guys talk to Corporal Swanson, I can't tell if you're talking about him or the tank. Calling him Dog and everything."

Wade rubbed his chin. "A new nickname would be in order. Any ideas?"

"Champ," Swanson suggested. "King. Captain America. Take your pick."

"Rock," said Russo. "Thorn."

"I like them names, Mac."

"As in a rock in my shoe. A thorn in my side."

"They still work for me."

"He's half man, half animal," Wade mused. "Beast

Man?"

"Manimal," Ackley said.

The crew laughed.

"That's giving him too much credit. How about just Animal?"

The tankers decided it with a cheer.

Swanson shrugged. "I don't care what you call me as long as you shut up while you're doing it. Time to show your cards, Mac."

Russo showed his cards. "Pair of jacks, Animal."

Ackley threw his down. "I ain't got a bit of luck."

"Three of a kind," Swanson gloated as he revealed his own cards. "Read 'em and weep. What about you, New Guy?"

Payne turned from the window and showed his hand. "I have a straight."

"Goddamn it! I can read everybody except you."

The bog shrugged. "Maybe it's because I don't care if I win or lose."

"Who the hell plays poker and don't care about winning? It's, it's—"

"Un-American," Wade helped him out.

"Yeah. It ain't American."

"How do you read me?" Russo asked.

Swanson snorted. "The way your hands are always moving, I'd know what you was saying even if I was deaf, which I am partly thanks to your big mouth."

"It's how people talk. They don't insult you while playing pocket pool."

"I don't have any tells," Ackley said. "I'm cool as a cucumber."

Swanson snickered. "Sure thing, Ack-Ack."

Wade rested his book on his lap. "It's good to see you apply your cunning to something constructive instead of looking for ways to antagonize people."

"When you get a winning hand, Prof? You get this smug look like a kid handed a big ol' hobby horse on his birthday." The loader gave his best impression, and the men laughed.

Wade sighed and returned to *Gatsby*.

The troop train clawed along the sweltering coast toward Oran, stopping every day for physical training and every few days to give the men a lukewarm shower under the water tanker's spout. At night, they slept in foldout bunks. The tankers lounged in their skivvies, their sweat misting the air like a sauna. They smoked, played cards, sang bawdy songs, and read comic books.

After a month of this, the train finally rolled into Oran, engine stack panting.

Wade had witnessed the city's transformation during the American occupation, and just in the past two months, it had changed even more. Civilians and soldiers crowded the streets around the train station. The alliance's scale was evident in the variety of uniforms. British, American, French, Senegalese, and bearded Goums, which were Moroccan irregulars wearing French helmets and striped robes and carrying deadly curved knives.

Over the crowds, a billboard displayed a beautiful woman against a red background. DRINK COCA-COLA. DELICIOUS AND REFRESHING.

The men sighed at the image, but Payne scowled. "I'm not sure if we're fighting for liberty or so they can sell more Coca-Cola."

Swanson shouldered his musette bag. "Ain't it the same thing, New Guy?"

Captain Ratliff shoved through the milling tankers. "Listen up! We're going to the docks! Form up, and prepare to mount!"

Russo and Swanson cast their longing gazes in the direction of the Hotel Aletti, where prostitutes worked the bar. With so many soldiers pouring into the city for the operation, the brass wasn't taking any chances. The Big Red One had rampaged through Oran in May, looting wine shops and punching out rear-echelon soldiers. The result was lockdown that now was being doubly enforced. MPs directed traffic at the street corners and otherwise kept a sharp eye on the brave fighting men they feared might run amok and burn the city to the ground.

The tankers waited in the wilting heat while the tanks were offloaded.

Captain Ratliff bellowed: "Destroyers, mount up! On the double! Move your asses!"

The sweating men shuffled toward their tanks lined up beside the train. Wade climbed onto the sponson, which radiated heat waves. He dropped inside and gasped. It was like crawling into an oven set to bake. The thick, hot air was difficult to breathe. The sun's afterimage smoldered green in his vision. His sweaty ears squished against his headphones. He wanted the tank to roll and get this over with, but that's not how hurry up and wait worked.

At last, the tanks started their engines all down the line and sat idling.

"We're never getting there," Russo complained.

"Seeing as there's Germans waiting to shoot at us when we do, I don't see what the big hurry is, Shorty," Ackley said.

"Mac just likes to bitch," Swanson said. "A soldier that can't screw, he bitches instead." He eyed the back of Payne's helmeted head. "Except you, New Guy. Nothing seems to bother you. It's creepy."

"Everything bothers me," the bog said. "I hate everything about this. If I ever make it back home, I'm never leaving again. How's that?"

The loader nodded. "Good."

"Misery loves company," Ackley said. "Even if the company makes you even more miserable."

Swanson guffawed. "Good one, Ack-Ack."

"All Destroyer units, this is Destroyer Six," Captain Ratliff said over the radio. "We're rolling."

The company commander followed up with detailed instructions for the platoons to move toward the waterfront. Feeling lightheaded, Wade melted in the heat and daydreamed about lemonade cooled with ice cubes.

At last, the tanks stopped, and Ratliff ordered the men to dismount.

"More bullshit," Swanson said before anybody asked what was going on.

The tankers exited Dog and joined their comrades in a line facing tables behind which clerks checked their names off a list. Beyond the tables, an enormous, boxy landing craft lay moored in the water, its ramp lowered to the quay like a giant mouth.

It was an LST, which stood for *Landing Ship, Tank*, but the other tankers—who'd trained with one in Morocco—swore meant *Large, Slow Target*. More than three hundred feet long and fifty feet wide at the beam, the ship was recently added to the Navy and carried a company of tanks plus additional vehicles.

Beyond, the crests of other ships crowded the waterfront, adding the smells of exhaust and motor oil to the powerful briny stink. Seagulls screeched overhead like *Stukas*. A column of sunburned German prisoners marched past in khaki rags, swinging their arms smartly and singing as they headed to a prisoner of war ship that would take them to America.

Wade watched them go, feeling impressed and anxious and a little annoyed these proud men weren't broken.

"If you could talk to them, what would you say?" Russo asked.

"I'd thank them for not trying to kill me," Wade said.

Payne snapped a picture. "I'd ask them why they put their lives on the line just to inflict so much misery on an entire continent."

"I'd ask where the best brothels are in Berlin," Swanson chimed in.

Russo guffawed. "What about you, Ack-Ack?"

"I wouldn't say anything," Ackley said. "They don't speak American."

"Good ol' Ackley. The fun-killer."

The whole crew burst out laughing this time. The line nudged forward until the clerks checked Wade's name off. This done, the crew returned to Dog. Tankers crowded around to admire the artwork Payne had painted on the platoon's other tanks at their request, especially Delilah in all her pinup glory. Their admiration gave Second Platoon a little extra swagger, like they were an elite unit.

Standing ramrod straight with a stiff back and a stiffer upper lip, a British liaison officer hailed them from the dock. "Sand in your shoes, Yanks!"

The tankers cheered in response to this traditional Desert Rat wish for good luck and good hunting. Finally, these men were going somewhere they might see action for the first time.

One stuck up his index finger. "We're gonna kick some Axis ass!"

"Not this again," Wade muttered. At Sidi bou Zid, the Germans had cured him of any overconfidence he might have had.

"Second Platoon, mount up," Lieutenant Pierce called out. "Prepare to board."

One by one, the vehicles reversed up the ramp into the landing ship's maw and parked in its cavernous interior. After nudging Dog into position, its crew took to the ladders to escape the engine exhaust choking the ventilation system and take in the view topside.

Freighters, frigates, transports, minesweepers, and landing craft crowded the harbor and its piers. Bosuns piped to welcome senior officers aboard their vessels.

Lines of infantry stomped across gangplanks. Gantry cranes swung cargo off the wharves and onto ships. Everywhere, sailors and soldiers shouted at each other. It was all a glorious mess, everybody busy but few knowing what they were doing and why.

Below them, the ramp groaned shut on retracting chains. The rumbling engines pulsed through the ship's metal flesh. The last tanks had been loaded. Blasting its horn, the ship eased away from the quay and steamed across the harbor through dozens of ships' chaotic wakes. There, it joined a cluster of other vessels awaiting exit to the open sea.

A sailor in a blue shirt and dungarees walked up to hand everybody a Mae West, small bottle of brandy, and some yellow anti-malaria pills that Wade knew from experience turned your skin orange.

"This is looking to be a nice trip." Swanson twisted his brandy's cap and raised it in a toast. "Who loves not women, wine, and song, will be a fool his whole life long." He gulped it down.

"That was for the seasickness, dumbass," the sailor said and moved on.

The loader shrugged. There was plenty more where that came from. They'd spent the last week filling Dog's every nook and cranny with bottles. One thing they'd learned about combat was they could never have enough liquid courage.

Another sailor approached with a bulging canvas bag. "Mail call. What's your platoon?" Wade answered him, and the sailor fished in the bag and passed out letters. Wade received three.

One was from a student at his university; another was from his parents.

The third was from his wife.

Despite the heat, he shivered at a thrill of longing. His stomach flipped in sudden turmoil. He'd done so well at compartmentalizing his marriage. By putting it on hold, he'd thought he'd solved it.

Alice had just reminded him it wasn't solved. It was still very much a part of him and now very much present.

Maybe she wants me back, he thought with a mix of hope and dread.

Maybe she wants a divorce.

"Wade?"

He wrenched his eyes from the envelope and gaped at Russo. Flipping back to the war gave him a touch of vertigo. "What?"

"Listen up." Russo turned from the gunwale to face his crew with his hands on his hips. "I just wanted to say something to you men. Something important. This is the start of a big one, and I wanted to tell you I'm proud—"

"Shut up, Mac," Swanson said.

They all stared at the hazy blue Mediterranean, where a journey awaited that would take them back to the war.

"Fun-killer," Russo muttered under his breath.

Wade looked down at the envelope in his hand, written by perhaps the biggest fun-killer of all, and wondered what it had in store for him.

CHAPTER FOUR

GRACIE, NAZI

Corporal Amos Swanson hated boats.

It wasn't because of seasickness. On the long voyage to Ireland aboard the *Queen Mary* and the jaunt to North Africa, he hadn't turned green once. What he hated was the openness of the sea.

Swanson came from hill folk, people who lived in a wrinkled land of hollers and copses where every hill and gully had a name. Plenty of places to dig in and hide. He felt safest enclosed, which made him suited for tank fighting. If he'd wound up in the Navy, he would have beelined for submarine service.

Still, it was cooler where he stood on the weather deck, and the sailors were less likely to harass him with requests to work. He laughed at the idea of doing cabin boy slopwork for a bunch of swabbies. These squids just didn't know Amos Swanson.

The sun blazed across a calm, azure Mediterranean that was speckled with ship formations stretching to the horizon in all directions. Barrage balloons hovered over the ships to deter enemy planes. Escort fighters lazily plowed the sky. Gazing at its scale, Swanson couldn't help but be impressed by the fleet's apparent strength. Classical music played over the ship's loudspeakers, *Charles Wade music*, he called it, though privately, he liked it.

He wondered how he'd ever explain these sights to the folks back home.

"Animal!" Chest puffed out, Russo strutted up like the rooster he was. "Did you hear the news?"

Swanson had heard they were going to Crete, that the Germans had landed paratroopers on Malta, and that U-boats had sunk half the invasion fleet, none of which he believed. He took his time lighting a Chesterfield. "Nope."

The tank commander grinned and handed him a booklet. Swanson stared at it. He didn't read well, and nobody ever handed him books. Then he noticed the ugly design and typesetting and knew the Army had made it.

"Sicily," Russo said.

Swanson took the booklet and slowly, painfully read aloud, "*Soldier's Guide to Sicily.* Ain't that where you're from?"

"*Coretta.* Syracuse."

"So we'll be shooting at your people, and here you are happy about it. You're an odd duck, Mac."

"I'll be liberating them from a tyrant. It was Mussolini that drove my family to come to America. We're going to take it back from him. When it's all over, I hope to visit them."

Swanson took a drag on his Chesterfield and blew a stream of smoke. "So I can thank Mussolini for having you in my life. Remind me to put that in my top five reasons under *Why We Fight.*"

"Can you stop being a bastard for five minutes?"

"I thought you knew me."

The rest of Dog's crew gathered at the gunwale. Payne produced his own cigarette pack and lit up. Even on a big ship, it was impossible to get away from these guys. As if they didn't get enough of each other stuffed into a tank.

"Looks like we all lost the pool," Wade said. "It isn't Sardinia like I thought."

Swanson grinned. "Who says I lost?"

Russo balked, apparently impressed. "How'd you know?"

He fixed his grin on Wade. "The Professor said it was obvious we'd be going to Sicily. Then he overthought it."

The gunner scowled and shook his head with frustration. Finally, he chuckled. "Okay. I guess I did."

"So what's this book say?"

"You aren't going to read it?"

"Unless it tells me how to ask for sex in Italian, I ain't interested."

As if to mark the revelation of the invasion's target, the classical tune stopped with a scratch. A moment later, "The Boogie Woogie Bugle Boy of Company B" blared over the loudspeakers. Sailors and tankers alike cheered at the change in music.

Wade flipped through the pages, skimming. "About the size of Vermont... Citrus orchards, olive plantations... Coastline a thousand kilometers in length, plenty of beaches in the south and west, where we'll probably be landing. Money's the *lire*. Hot as hell, swamps, malaria, sandfly fever, typhoid, typhus."

"Sounds like another shithole," Ackley said.

"Hey," Russo warned.

"I'm just wondering why we can't invade a nice place. Beautiful girls in swimsuits and plenty of beer to go around."

"That'd be nice," Payne agreed with a smile. "Maybe next time we'll invade California."

"You'll see plenty of beautiful girls in Sicily," Russo promised.

"Wow, listen to this," Wade went on. "'An American report maintains that gangsterism in the USA had its origin in Sicilian immigration.'"

"Ha!" Swanson said.

"'Ha,' says the guy whose family were moonshine runners," Russo shot back.

Wade went on, "It says the island's been invaded many times in the past. That I know to be true. It bodes well for us."

"Ha!" Swanson said again. "A bunch of pushovers. Even the Army says so. All sand, no iron."

Russo was turning purple. "I'll show you some iron knuckles anytime you want, *bisgott*."

Wade ignored them. "Who wrote this thing? Listen to this: 'Morals are superficially very rigid, being based on the Catholic religion...' But 'they are, in actual fact, of a very low standard, particularly in the agricultural areas.'"

Swanson flicked the remains of his cigarette overboard. "Now *that* bodes well for us. Finally, something useful."

"Then it says this: The Sicilian is 'well known for his extreme jealousy insofar as his womenfolk are concerned, and in a crisis still resorts to a dagger.' That doesn't bode so well for you, Animal."

"Been there, done that," Swanson said. "So how does a guy ask for sex, Mac?"

"*M'av'a scusari*," Russo said. "Say that and they open right up."

"Wait until they get a load of a real man," he said, though he wondered if Russo was putting him on.

"Another word you'll want to know is *vino*," Wade said. "Which is wine." He chuckled. "Here's a couple of words you should learn in any language, Animal. *Prego*, which is *please*. And *gracie*, which is *thank you*."

"*Gracie*, Nazi," Swanson said. "*Prego*, Dago. Easy to remember."

"One of these days," Russo growled.

The song ended. The loudspeakers blatted. Captain Ratliff's voice filled the air: "This is a message from the boss himself, General George Patton. 'We are now on our way to force a landing on the coast of Sicily. Our immediate mission is to capture a beachhead and the coastal cities of Licata, Gela, and Scoglitti. Once this is accomplished, we will move toward Messina, destroying any Axis forces that oppose us. Joining us in this noble endeavor is the justly famous Eighth Army, which attacks on our right.

"'When we land, we will meet German and Italian soldiers whom it is our honor and privilege to attack and destroy.

"'Many of you have in your veins German and Italian blood, but remember that these ancestors of yours so loved freedom that they gave up home and country to cross the ocean in search of liberty.'"

"*La vesa gazi*," Russo muttered. "This again."

Swanson chuckled at him, mostly because he could.

"'Remember that we as attackers have the initiative. We must retain this tremendous advantage by always attacking rapidly, ruthlessly, viciously, without rest. However tired and hungry you may be, the enemy will be more tired, more hungry. Keep punching. God is with us. We shall win.' Message ends."

After a short pause, the captain added, "Per the regular schedule, after noon chow, all Army personnel will line up on the second deck to take their anti-malaria medication. That is all."

A week later, the fleet had merged with other fleets to form a vast armada covering the sea, some three thousand ships, the sailors' scuttlebutt said. Three times more than Helen of Troy's face launched, according to the Professor.

Aboard the USN LST *Chippewa County*, the tankers had reverted back to the wild. In their sweltering quarters, where they hot-bunked on beds sardine-stacked four high, the men endured stopped toilets, petty theft, and weevils in the chow. With no showers, they were sweaty and grimy and ripe. Thriving gambling rings and black markets sprang up, where money changed hands and violence was doled out for debts unpaid.

With the ship sealed up tight for the night, the tankers lay in their bunks and hammocks or sat on the deck among heaps of stacked weapons and equipment.

They wrote letters home, played dice in the stairwells, and stared at the bulkheads in dread of the coming landings. Somebody had a stolen radio tuned to Axis Sally, a favorite among the tankers because she always played swing between her anti-Roosevelt and anti-Jewish propaganda. While she spun one of Swanson's favorite tunes, "Smoke Gets in Your Eyes," the ship rocked more than usual. Word spread of a mighty wind building topside, a Mussolini wind.

While Swanson lay in his bunk trying to sleep through this heaving sauna, Russo pontificated to the crew about the new pontoon bridges the Navy had cooked up. Despite the man's naturally elevated volume, Swanson was able to tune him out.

Wade, meanwhile, moped on the opposite bunk, reading and re-reading his mysterious letter from his wife, just as he had all week. It made Swanson curious but not enough to task. He liked the Professor quiet, though he had to admit it wasn't as fun when he was.

"The LST is going to land us on the beach in front of Gela," Russo said, as if they didn't already know. "If we run into an unexpected sandbar, they'll bolt together the floating pontoon and run it to the shore to make a causeway."

"Sounds very safe," Ackley said, pure sarcasm.

"Well, the thing is, it's never been tested."

"It's being tested all right. By us rolling over it with a thirty-ton—"

Across their quarters, men cursed as the square-bowed, flat-bottomed ship banged against a large swell. Ackley and Russo stumbled into the bunks and fell in a dog pile on Swanson, who cursed and shoved at them.

Ackley regained his footing and turned green as the ship banged against the next swell. "Well, all right—"

He vomited onto the deck, splashing Swanson's bunk.

"Get a goddamn bucket," Swanson yelled.

This wasn't FUBAR, which stood for *fucked up beyond all recognition*. This was FUAFUP, *fucked up and fucked up proper*.

The ship lurched again and paused in an alarming list that sent weapons and equipment and anything else not bolted down rattling across the deck. Axis Sally died with a crash. Water splashed into their quarters from above and washed the deck with a tiny roller. Booms and chains broke free and clattered against the upper decks. The entire ship seemed to be coming apart.

As the deck went on rolling, Swanson suddenly didn't feel so good himself.

I don't get seasick, he thought as the contents of his stomach shot up his throat. He leaned over the bunk just in time.

The ship listed again as if threatening to capsize, but Swanson was too sick to care about the prospect of drowning.

So much for God being on our side, he thought as he spat.

While *Chippewa County*'s sailors fought the raging gale on the weather decks, the men of Destroyer Company hurled and cried without relief.

July 10. Invasion.

Wet and reeking and with life jackets around their necks, the tankers lined the gunwales topside to watch the bombardment. The Mussolini wind had leveled off to a cool breeze that to Swanson proved a welcome relief after more than a day of tumbling around the ship's foul, sweltering bowels.

Surrounded by other ships' red and green navigation lights, the LST and its sisters zigzagged in the dark while a screen of fast-moving destroyers guarded against U-boat attack. Humming through the night, escort fighters secured the air overhead.

As Swanson understood it, the plan was to land Seventh Army along a ten-mile stretch of coast. Task Force Joss, consisting of the 3rd Infantry Division, was the attack's west wing and would land at Licata. Task Force Dime, consisting of the Big Red One, would take the central prize, the fishing village of Gela. And Task Force Cent, consisting of the 45th Infantry, would take Scoglitti in the east. 2nd Armored would act as reserve and support the three groups; Swanson's company would land as part of Dime. Meanwhile, the British and Canadians would make their own landings in southeastern Sicily.

After establishing the beachhead, the goal was to push northeast toward Messina on the island's northeastern tip, where a two-mile strait separated it from the Italian boot. Once Messina was captured, all Axis forces would be trapped and destroyed, and the Allies could count another win.

And here was Corporal Amos Swanson, a tiny wheel in a vast, floundering, chaotic war machine now being unleashed. All to capture a dumb island that, compared to the vastness of Europe, was a pebble.

Destroyers and cruisers opened fire with flashes that bleached the sky. The men flinched as the first blasts concussed the atmosphere. The shells hurtled toward the shoreline in a hellish chorus of howls.

With piercing booms, domes of white light throbbed along the coast until melting yellow and winking out. Soon, the entire waterfront blazed. Fires glowed red on the horizon, silhouetting the town of Gela and its beaches.

"*Minch!*" Russo shouted over the din. "What a show!"

After an hour of this, Ackley shook his head in disbelief. "How can anybody survive that?"

The prowling destroyers swept the shore with searchlights, looking for more targets. The first landing craft and transports churned across the whitecaps toward the beaches. Swanson spotted their lumbering outlines leading phosphorescent wakes.

A powerful searchlight on the shore switched on and flashed past the LST before settling on one of the approaching infantry landing craft. Machine guns rattled in pillboxes on the beach, their tracers streaming across the water.

A destroyer zeroed in on the searchlight and fired its five-inch guns until it winked out. More machine guns were firing now, joined by mortars and coastal guns that punched hills and geysers from the sea.

"Looks like plenty of guys survived it," Swanson said. "Standing their ground too."

"They would." Russo set his jaw. "They're Italians."

A blinding burst of light rippled across the water with a resounding crash, leaving a massive cloud of dust hanging over the rollers.

"That's the pier," Wade said. "The Italians just blew it up so we couldn't use it."

Shells ripped across Gela, shattering houses and hurling silhouetted debris as the landing craft groped toward it. The men tensed at the gunwales as a fierce battle erupted all along the beach. The rangers had begun their assault, followed by waves of general infantry from the Big Red One.

The tanks were scheduled to go ashore once the infantry secured a beachhead. If the doughs failed, 2nd Armored wasn't going anywhere.

"Come on," Russo breathed, though Swanson wasn't entirely sure whom he was rooting for at the moment.

The shooting flared and waned for an hour until it sputtered out. The landing craft returned to the fleet to make way for the next wave.

"Looks like we did it," Wade said.

"Well, that was easy," Ackley said in wonder.

"It isn't over yet."

It seemed to be. The shoreline smoldered like a bed of coals. Otherwise, aside from the random spark of gunfire, there wasn't much to see. The battle appeared to be finished.

Wade added, "It'll be our turn soon enough."

"It'll be worth it," Swanson said. "Just to get off this goddamn tub."

Against blackout orders, he sat on the deck and

lit a cigarette. The operation was SUSFU—*situation unchanged, still fucked up*—and the tanks were going in at first light. He thought he should get some shuteye while he could, but that meant returning to his quarters' oven heat. The night air was warm, but it wasn't sweltering, and it didn't stink of vomit, sweat, and stopped-up toilets.

He tossed his butt overboard, closed his eyes, and fell asleep where he sat, even with the heart-stopping crashes of the unending Navy bombardment.

A hand shook him awake.

Swanson blinked at the pale yellow sky but couldn't find the sun. He rubbed his eyes and tried again, with the same result.

The air filled with the howl of planes and chatter of flak guns.

"What the hell's going on?" he said.

"The hard part has started," Wade told him. "The fleet's under attack."

"Seems so," the loader growled with irritation, part of him blaming his comrades for all this, as if they'd allowed the attack just to wake him up.

I go to sleep for five lousy minutes...

He rose to take in the horror show unfolding for miles all around him. Axis planes had dropped magnesium flares that floated toward the earth on parachutes. In the glaring light, they dove through countless streams of flak to strafe and bomb the invasion fleet. Two miles distant, a minesweeper blazed on the water while other ships smoked from battle damage.

SICILY

It was like a motion picture, only it wasn't. With a picture, Swanson knew the story that tied it all together. Some of the good guys might die, but they always won.

In a real battle, he saw only fragments. Bombs erupted along a destroyer's deck. A strafing run sparked off a cruiser's forecastle. Streaming smoke, a plane angled toward the sea, breaking apart in tumbling pieces. Barrage balloons sank in mini infernos. Depth charges boomed underwater as the destroyers battled a wolf pack of U-boats.

And none of it meant anything. There was no narrative, no moral, no certainty of outcome. Anything could happen.

Swanson became very aware he stood on top of a giant floating box with five hundred tons of metal in its belly, just a few miles from a smoldering shoreline where crazy Italians waited with machine guns.

In the east, a pale glow framed the horizon. Dawn was coming fast. He hadn't been asleep for five minutes but several hours. Soon, the whistles would blow and he'd be ordered to mount Dog and drive straight into whatever nightmare awaited him ashore.

It ain't fair, he thought, feeling sorry for himself.

The air turned a blinding white. The detonation that followed a moment later rent the atmosphere and flattened his eardrums.

This is it!

He emerged gasping and patted himself to make sure he was still there. His heart galloped in his chest. His ears ringing with a deafening hum, he barked a laugh, and the crew joined in. The laughter of the insane.

A ship nearby had blown up. Pieces of it were still raining down in thousands of splashes off *Chippewa County*'s beam.

The LST's loudspeakers blared, "Now hear this, now hear this. Tankers, go to your assembly area. Tankers, go to your assembly area."

Swanson's bowels liquefied as the men shuffled to the ladders in silence.

This small-town West Virginia mountain boy, who'd already been to Ireland and three countries in North Africa, was about to invade Italy.

CHAPTER FIVE

SAFU

On the well deck, Corporal Russo paced through puddles remaining after the storm flood. The tanks and support vehicles stood in their rows, waterproofed with hooded exhausts, air intake stacks sealed with shrouds, and gun barrels taped up nice and tight. The LST's giant twin engines filled the cavernous space with their dull roar. Water misted in the air. The concussion of the Navy's big guns thudded through the bulkheads.

"Hurry up and wait," Swanson growled. Smoking one of his Chesterfields, the loader sprawled on the rear deck among the piled gear. "*Hurry up* and *waaaaaait.*"

"Our situational awareness is limited," Russo told him. "We have—"

"And waaaaaait."

He cleared his throat. "We have to trust—"

"Waaaaaaaa—"

"—in command. You know that—"

"—*aaaaaaaaaaaaaaaaait.*"

"—war is one percent fighting, nine percent moving, and ninety percent waiting."

"Wait," Swanson grated, just to get the last word.

Russo sighed. He was the tank commander, but he was no John Austin. The men respected him in the cupola but otherwise enjoyed antagonizing him as they had when he was doing the driving.

Without Austin, the tank crew was a looser bunch, a little less wound up and likely to act out on each other, but something important had been lost. Discipline, maybe. A singular purpose driven by one man's leadership. Austin had been able to push the men to be better as a team than they were as individuals.

Once Dog rolled onto that beach, Russo would have to make decisions that meant the crew's life or death. In battle, he was responsible for them, and they'd be responsible to each other. However, he wanted to inspire them somehow now.

"Men, we've been through a lot of shit together."

The men all gazed at him from where they sat or lay on the tank's armor.

Good, he thought. *They're listening.*

"And we're about to go through a whole lot more. But I know we can win this one. The country's counting on us. When the great evil of fascism—"

"We were safer topside," Ackley cut him off. "Speaking of going through a lot of shit. Up there, we can swim if the Krauts sink us. Down here, we're just waiting to get ourselves drowned."

Russo fixed him with the evil eye. "I was trying to take everybody's mind off that, *chooch*. But here's what's gonna happen, since you can't wait to fight your war. The minute this ship heads to land, every Axis plane in the sky is gonna try to drop an egg on us, and it won't matter where you're standing."

The men stiffened, their eyes alert. He had their full attention now.

"Assuming we survive that, best case is the ship drops anchor and slides right on the beach, which is too soft to drive on, infested with mines, and getting pounded by arty," he gloated. "Worst case, we get hung up on a sandbar and sit there while the pontoon bridge is set up, a bridge that's never been tested in combat."

Ackley scowled. "You don't have to sugar coat it—"

"We make it through all that, we'll have the privilege of getting shot at. And so what? Do your job and do it well, or you're dead and so is the rest of your crew. Me, I intend to make it home in one piece, *capish*?"

"Me, I actually don't care when we go, *Duce*," Swanson said. "I hope they make us wait all year. We're just bitching to pass the time. But it's good to see you talking turkey like a real commander for once instead of cheerleading."

"I liked his first speech better," Butch called from Dealer, the tank he commanded. "I hate Nazis. Kill 'em all."

Sergeant Cranston laughed from Duck Soup. "I tell my guys that the sooner they win this thing, the sooner they'll have grateful Sicilian gals all over them."

Toking on his pipe, Lieutenant Pierce leaned against Delilah. "Which they can't do a damn thing about, given the rules against fraternizing. Don't promise what you can't give."

"Come on, sir," Cranston said. "You know what Patton said."

The tankers burst with a ragged shout, "'An army that can't fuck won't fight!'"

Pierce shook his head. "Don't let me see you trying

is all I have to say."

"They should make you the company commander, Shorty," Ackley said. "Because every time you talk, the whole company hears it."

Russo stalked off, but there was nowhere to go, nowhere to be alone. In the Army, the latrine was the only place you could go to be by yourself, and even then some guy was sitting beside you asking if you'd brought a pinup to share or could pass a roll of TP.

He mounted the sponson, stepped over Swanson, and dropped into the cupola. He closed the hatch behind him and sighed.

Alone at last. Quieter too.

Wade dropped into the turret through the loader's hatch. "Hey, Tony."

"Hey."

"You got this."

Russo patted his breast pocket and felt the reassuring lump of John Austin's Revolutionary War bullet, which the men in his family had carried into combat in every American conflict since. "Austin made it look a whole lot easier."

"It doesn't matter how it looks." Wade settled into the loader's seat. "If I cared how things look, I'd be the commander. You're the commander because I'm best on the gun and you're a good man to have in the cupola."

"If Animal or Ack-Ack were commanding, I'd surrender to the nearest Axis unit."

Wade chuckled. "That goes without saying. The point is the only thing that matters to me is maximizing our odds of survival. In other words, to put it crassly, *my* survival. Me putting you in command shows how much trust I have in you."

Russo turned away to hide his smile. "I guess so."

"Do you mind if I give you a bit of advice, though?"

"Sure."

"You get shit from the crew, you don't get steamed and walk off," the gunner said. "You eat it. If you can't take Ackley or Swanson, how will you handle combat? It sends a bad message."

"It's a lot more than I thought it was going to be," Russo confessed. "Being responsible for four other guys. It gets in my head sometimes."

"Just be responsible for yourself. Do every single thing in combat thinking about how you're going to survive and how you're going to kill to survive. You do that, you'll do all right, and we'll be right there with you."

Russo grinned. It all made sense to him. "Thanks, Charles."

"Don't mention it."

"This was a good talk. I hope you'll always give it to me straight."

Wade eyed him in the gloom. "Oh, I will. Since your survival directly affects mine, you can count on it."

The LST held station off Sicily's southern coast. The hours rolled by until the thuds of outgoing shells became mere background noise.

While the tank company idled, the LST's sailors shared news, none of it good. Due to vehicles crowding the beach, landing craft waited hours to be unloaded. Frequent air attacks and artillery fire damaged or destroyed increasing numbers of landing craft. Unexpected sandbars paralleling the beach blocked bigger craft from landing, and a pontoon bridge had to be erected.

The invasion had gone SAFU—a *self-adjusting fuckup*.

Russo inspected his crew. The chatter had died down to a funereal silence. The men were haggard. They'd endured over a week of confinement in a sweaty box, more than a day of being tossed by a gale, and a tense, sleepless night. They were getting used up before they even hit the beach. Tired men made mistakes, and mistakes got men killed.

After the sailors served a cold supper and changed the waste buckets, he whistled for his crew's attention.

"Not this again," Swanson said.

Russo gave them all a hard-eyed stare. "We may be here a while longer. Let's make the best of it and get some sleep."

The men nodded and jumped down to the deck to untie their bedrolls.

"What's with these logs tied on the tank?" Payne asked.

"We put them there to get the new guys to ask about them," Swanson said.

"Something we learned in Algeria," Wade explained. "We got the whole platoon to get their own. You lay them—"

"Now hear this, now hear this," the loudspeakers

called. "Tankers, man your tanks. Tankers, man your tanks."

Russo glared at the nearest speaker, thinking, *This had better be for real.* "All right, mount up!"

The men settled into their stations and plugged their headsets into the control boxes. Swanson switched on the radio transmitter and receiver then pressed their assigned channel button until it locked.

Russo selected INT on the radio. "Check interphone!"

"Gunner, check."

"Bog, check."

"Driver, check."

"Hurry up and wait," Swanson said.

"Destroyers 2, this is Destroyers 2 Actual," Lieutenant Pierce said over the radio. "The LST has veered to land. Wait for the signal to start tanks."

The men clenched at their stations, but the disembark order did not come.

"Destroyers 2, this is Destroyers 2 Actual," Pierce said.

"Don't even say it," Russo muttered.

"We have a couple of LSTs ahead of us waiting to offload onto the pontoon bridge. Our turn will come soon enough. Out."

The ship trembled as the booms outside intensified. This wasn't five-inch shells lobbed at shore targets; this was incoming. Even through the bulkheads and tank's armor, Russo heard the howl of diving planes.

The LST listed from a near miss. Shock waves walloped the hull.

"I changed my mind," Swanson said. "I'd be happy to go straight into combat just to get off this goddamn boat."

A resounding crash shook the LST.

"Our father, who art in heaven," Russo murmured in prayer. His mind blanked on the rest. He hoped God got the idea.

"Destroyers 2, uh, that was the ammo in the LST ahead of us going up." The lieutenant's voice sounded thin and shaky. "The pontoon bridge is gone."

The men bowed their heads as if to engage the almighty in their own prayers.

"Pick one," Wade muttered. "Coming or going. Coming or going. Pick one."

"Bad news ashore," Pierce added. "The doughs ran into Kraut armor. They're asking for tank support. Our ship's skipper is looking for a way around the sandbar."

"The skipper's lost his marbles," Ackley said.

Payne opened his bog hatch, leaned over the side, and vomited.

"Don't you puke on my tank, New Guy," Swanson said.

The hatch shut. "Sorry about that."

"Nothing to be sorry about," Russo said. He transmitted, "Two Actual, this is 2-5. Any ID on the Kraut armor we might be rolling up against?"

"Wait, one." The radio came back, "The Hermann Göring Division."

"The Luftwaffe's very own elite mechanized force," Wade said. "I think I'm going to puke next."

Despite his own fear, Russo knew what he had to

do. "Men, on this day, this day of days, I'm proud to lead you into combat and put the axe to the Axis. The eyes of our great nation, no, the world—"

The interphone exploded with curses.

"Where's the Tommy?" Swanson fumed. "I'm gonna accidentally discharge my toes off."

Wade turned at his station and made eye contact with Russo.

"Bada bing." Russo winked.

The gunner smiled and returned to the 75.

"Destroyers 2, this is Destroyers 2 Actual," the radio blatted. "The LST maneuvered us through, but we'll be landing a good two miles south of the landing zone they designated us. All tanks, crank your engines."

"On it," Ackley said and climbed out.

Russo switched to RADIO. "Two Actual, this is 2-5. What kind of reception are we rolling into? Should we put one in the gun?"

"Prepare for every type of FU you can imagine," came the answer. "No hostile ground forces on the beach, though. Negative on loading the guns. But eyes sharp, and be ready for anything."

"Roger that, sir."

The LST's squared bow banged on the rollers as they drew near the shore.

"Thirty seconds," the loudspeakers blared. "God be with you men."

"All tanks, start your engines," Pierce ordered. "Prepare to disembark."

Ackley climbed back into the driver's seat and ignited Dog's big aviation engine, which growled to life.

Russo sweated in the cupola, waiting for the go order. "Driver, standby to move out."

The priority was to get off the beach as quickly as possible to make way for the next unit. Pierce would tell him where to go, and the beach master would tell the lieutenant where to go. It was nighttime, and he was second in line. All Ackley had to do was follow Delilah's hooded red tail lights.

The LST dropped its stern anchor to speed its deceleration. Moments later, the bulkheads trembled as the bow plowed into the sand and settled.

The ramp fell, revealing the beachhead in utter confusion. Everywhere, men ran among stacked and scattered equipment and vehicles. The Jericho trumpet sirens of Stukas filled the night with blood-curdling banshee howls. Their bombs fell in blinding fireballs that flung tons of debris down the beach.

"Geronimo!" Pierce yelled as sand and equipment rained across the water.

Something else was wrong. The beach was too far away—

Delilah lunged off the ramp with a mighty splash.

The water was nine feet deep at the heavy surf's crest. The tank sank almost all the way up to the commander's hatch. Luckily, the waterproofing held, and Delilah rolled through the swelling waves toward the shore.

"*Maronna mia*," Russo breathed. "Driver, move out! Stay on Delilah!"

Dog plunged into the sea. Ahead, Delilah was still rolling. He reached over the side of the turret and pulled his hand away soaked to the wrist.

"*Maronna mia*," he muttered again.

"What the hell?" Ackley shouted. "We're underwater! I'm driving blind!"

If the tank stalled and got hit by a big wave, Dog would be a write-off.

"Just keep driving, Ackley! I'll be your eyes! Go, go, go!"

Minutes later, Dog growled out of the surf pouring water and rode up onto the shingle. In the thick, humid night air, five-inch shells hurtled overhead and pounded the interior. The glowing red skyline silhouetted the distant town on its limestone hill. A wave of smoke passed over the scene.

A landing ship blazed on the water, illuminating a coastline full of junk scattered on the sand and tumbling in the chaotic waves. Men screamed from the shadows for a medic.

Payne opened his hatch and looked around. "Jesus God. What the hell is this?"

"Out of the fire into the fire, New Guy," said Swanson.

To Russo, it looked like another case of the generals throwing spaghetti against the wall and hoping it all stuck. Pierce hadn't been kidding when he'd said the beachhead had reached a point of every type of FU one could imagine.

"Driver, stay on Delilah." He hoped his tone projected calm.

Delilah drove through the helter-skelter of the beach and up the gentle rise toward a row of sand dunes. Dog followed, its tracks crunching the wet sand and stone of the shingle.

Russo spared a glance behind him. Everywhere he looked, landing craft burned, had capsized, or lay on their sides on the beach. Flashes popped along the horizon, followed moments later by the ghostly runaway-train crashes of the big shells screaming overhead. One of the big ships had been hit and was aflame. Sparks flickered in the sky, marking a string of dogfights.

Soon, the tanks would be off the beach. Then they'd wait again, this time for the rest of the battalion to show up. Plenty of hours to ponder taking on the Hermann Göring Division in the—

Dog shuddered to a halt, its engine whining.

Ahead of them, Delilah lurched to the side as it crested a dune, churning sand until its own engines howled.

"We're stuck," Ackley said.

They were bogged in the beach's soft sand.

CHAPTER SIX

COUNTERATTACK

Dawn revealed the wreckage of the American beachhead. PFC Payne scanned a thousand yards of sand dunes, which led up to rolling hills.

So near, yet so far.

Forty to eighty feet tall and dotted with scrub, these dunes had stopped Destroyer Company's armored vehicles cold. Half the company had either thrown tracks or bellied in the soft sand. Payne had helped dig Dog out, but they weren't going anywhere. For now, they were trapped on this beach.

Guns thundered a few miles north. The 26th Infantry Regiment had pushed out from Gela and was engaged in a fierce battle. Most likely screaming for tank support that still wasn't coming.

Payne turned toward the sea. Capsized boats, gas masks, life vests, and other gear and ordnance lay strewn across the beachfront among haphazardly heaped supply crates. Drifting clouds of black smoke smudged the brightening sky. Bogged trucks and vehicles stood abandoned. Several burned-out halftracks lay scattered on the sand, where they'd run into Teller mines. In the water, tugs struggled to refloat a sunken LST.

Then he allowed himself to see the bodies. They were everywhere, scattered and awaiting removal by

Graves Registration, sometimes whole and bloodless like something out of a motion picture, other times naked or scattered in pieces. Many were half buried, torsos and hands and helmeted heads protruding from sandy mounds, as if the beach was a sloppily dug mass grave.

This wasn't what Payne had expected. In his imagination, war was a direct and almost elegant affair. Both sides showed up and fought it out, and then one army executed a powerful and creative maneuver to defeat the other.

So far, the real thing involved combating climate and geography far more than the Axis. The apparent strategy was to vomit men and equipment onto a ten-mile stretch of coast and shove them toward a series of objectives, shedding bodies and equipment along the way. If the armies came into contact, the battle would probably involve blind luck—having more men and materiel at the right place and right time—far more than strategic brilliance.

Captain Ratliff climbed the dune and clenched his teeth at the view. "We have to cross all that before the Heinies come back with their planes. We're sitting ducks in daylight."

"Yes, sir," Payne said, because there was nothing else to say.

"What's that camera doing around your neck? You think you're a tourist?"

"No, sir."

"You're the guy who painted your platoon's turrets."

"That's right, sir."

"Let's see how creative you are. Any bright ideas how to get off this beach?"

He thought about it. "Bangalore torpedoes?"

Ratliff's cold blue eyes bored into him. "Bangalores?"

"Blow a valley right through all this, drive straight through."

"Bangalores." The captain erupted in laughter. "Bangalores!" He turned to the tankers waiting below. "Unfuck this now. Bring up the steel road."

The men hauled spools of bent steel matting and unrolled them across the dune. A tank with DUKE painted on its side rumbled to life and crawled toward it until the treads bit on the mat.

Ratliff's plan was far simpler and more effective: Slap something down that provided traction and distributed the tank's weight.

Duke topped the dune, and its commander leaned out to give the men a thumbs up. The tankers cheered.

Payne was green but learning quickly. The only problem was he wasn't sure he wanted to learn any of this. War was turning out to be a vast labor just to have the chance to kill and be killed. Buster Jackson had it right. Payne would have been a hell of a lot more comfortable and safe peeling potatoes, and he'd have been far more useful.

The grating sound of shrieking metal made the men flinch. Duke's treads snarled the steel matting and dragged it around the bogie wheels. Engine groaning, the tank bucked and stopped cold.

"Maybe they have another one of those pontoon bridges," Payne said. "We could drape it across the dunes."

"Stick to painting." Red-faced, Ratliff whistled up another tank to take a turn on the steel road.

Payne trudged down the sand dune toward his waiting crew. Judging by the string of curses the captain let loose, the next tank had similar luck.

"Give us a hand here," Wade said.

The men unstrapped the logs from Dog's flanks and hauled them in front of the tank's treads.

"Traction," Payne guessed. These tankers hadn't trusted the newfangled steel road and relied instead on an old standby, which was logs.

"Put your back into it, New Guy," Swanson said, while doing nothing himself. "No shirking on our crew."

Payne bristled. Nobody ever called him lazy. Then he counted to ten in his head and blew out a sigh. He understood the loader needed to play the bully the same way Payne needed to paint. Over time, the world slowly went off-kilter, or he did—one or the other—but either way, painting leveled it all out again. Maybe it was how Swanson made sense of his world.

Best to let it go and ignore all the bullshit, or he'd end up buried to his neck in it.

Russo waved. "Give it a go, Ackley."

The red-haired kid pushed the sticks, and Dog edged forward. The tracks bit into the first log and rolled over it, then the next five. The tank crested the sand dune and settled on the other side triumphant.

"That was actually easy," Payne said.

Swanson's homely mug morphed into a sinister

grin. "Sure thing, New Guy. Now all we got to do is do that about thirty more times, and we'll be all done."

Payne crouched at one end of a log. "Well?"

"Well, what?"

"Let's get to it. Grab that end."

"Yeah, *chooch*," Russo said. "Put your back into it."

Swanson scowled but heaved at the log.

Behind Dog, the other tanks in the platoon laid out their own timber and were catching up.

Captain Ratliff glowered at them. "Put that down and listen up." He added with a shout, "All of you, listen up!"

The entire company gathered around.

"Here it is. The Heinies are coming in force. The whole goddamn Hermann Göring Division is on the move and hitting the 26th and the 16th hard. When I say hard, I mean the 26th is being overrun and is retreating back to Gela. To make things even more fun, the Livorno Division is coming at the town from the west. They're mountain troops, the best the ginzos got. They're all coming right at us, and their aim is to split the American beachhead in two."

"They have to get through us first!" a tanker called out to cheers.

"Like a warm knife through butter," Wade muttered under his breath.

"We're going to push out as far into the dunes as we can and form a firing line with whatever infantry we can scrape together," Ratliff told them. "Let's get it done."

The meeting broke up, and the men returned to

their tanks.

"For God's sake," Wade said. "It's Sidi bou Zid all over again. Outnumbered, outgunned, and the enemy has air superiority."

"Yeah, but don't forget that this time we've got the sea at our backs and nowhere to run," Russo said. "With only a single company instead of a battalion."

A motley collection of infantry marched past them into the dunes, a makeshift defense force composed of Army shore party engineers and Navy yeomen, quartermasters, and auxiliarymen. Every able man who could hold a gun was being called up to make a last-ditch stand.

Payne helped Swanson shift another log then nudged Russo. "Who's that?"

Wearing a determined, confident scowl, a man in a dress uniform climbed out of a staff car and swaggered across the beach. Several aides followed him, casting anxious glances at the sky.

As the man approached, Payne took in the lacquered helmet with its three big stars on the front, riding crop, breeches that flared at the thigh, binoculars and camera swinging from his neck, and holstered .45 revolvers on his hips.

"That," said Russo, "is General Patton."

"The commander of the whole army?"

"The guy who got us into this mess," Swanson growled.

Payne stiffened to attention and saluted as Patton marched up to him and glared directly into his face.

"Who the hell is in charge of this circus?" the

general fumed.

"You are, sir," Payne answered dutifully.

"Jesus God." Ratliff interposed himself before Payne said another word. "I'm the company commander, General."

"Then you can tell me what the hell you're doing sitting here with your thumb up your ass while the Boche are rolling over our boys out there!"

"The ground's too soft, General. It's slowing us down."

"Then get out and push!"

The captain blinked, unsure if Patton was serious. "Yes, sir."

"Push these men and get into the goddamn fight!" The general took in the company at a glance and settled on Payne's platoon. "I see one platoon had the brains to bring logs for a corduroy road." He squinted at Russo. "Do I know you?"

"Yes, sir, we met at a hospital in—"

The general raised his hand and turned back to Ratliff. "Get this platoon's big boys off the beach and up to Piano Lupo. And hold it. The rest of your company can catch up as fast as it can. Do you understand me, Captain?"

"Loud and..." Ratliff looked up with wide eyes.

"What's the matter with you? Cat got your tongue?"

Ratliff turned and howled, "Man your fifties and take cover!"

A Stuka hummed out of the rising sun. It waggled its wings, and two planes trailing it spread out into a diving formation. One after the other, the dive-bombers peeled off as tracers from the M4s' .50-caliber machine guns angled toward them. Payne stood stupidly out in the open watching the show, impressed by their bravado and sheer majesty.

The planes fell into screaming dives a mile south of the tanks and dropped their bombs on easier prey. Men, vehicles, and plumes of sand erupted from the beach. Another mile back a second trio of Stukas clobbered a landing craft, which reared from the water and sank in a sheet of spray.

"I had a dream I shot one of those planes down with my pistols."

Payne noticed the striking figure of General Patton standing beside him. Together, they were the only men who hadn't rushed to cover during the attack. The planes receding back into the sunrise, the tankers and Patton's entourage stood and dusted sand from their uniforms.

Payne said nothing. He didn't particularly like Patton. In his book, any man who'd order tanks and cavalry to attack Americans on American soil, as he had the Bonus Army, wasn't somebody to admire. Still, Payne now felt a strange kinship with this bulldog general.

Patton added, "Impressive, aren't they?"

"They are, General. Very impressive, actually."

"Do they frighten you, son? Or do they make you mad as hell?"

"I think both," Payne said.

War terrified him, but not because he thought he was going to die, at least not yet, anyway. Like the first time he'd seen a medium tank roll onto the training field back at Fort Knox, he found war ugly but compelling. Not that it was elegant. It wasn't at all. It was a horrible, raw, messy, dangerous spectacle.

One he nonetheless found beautiful, achingly beautiful.

And that scared him.

He believed the brave might fight a war for a just cause they judged was worth their lives, but only the insane admired it for any reason. That was the connection he felt with this grizzled warhorse.

"Both," Patton echoed.

"Yes, sir."

"That is an acceptable answer. In fact, it's the only answer." The general glared over his shoulder as he stomped off to his staff car. "Now get out there and kill the bastards!"

Payne watched Patton drive toward Gela and wondered if being a soldier made one crazy, or if being crazy made one a good soldier.

Again, he decided it was both.

CHAPTER SEVEN

SURPRISE PARTY

The sweating men groaned as they hustled the logs in front of Second Platoon's tanks like laborers laying track in front of an impatient train. Tank Sergeant Wade took it all in through his periscope and sighed.

His steady advance to battle Göring's panzers had a terrible inevitability to it. The company cut off from its battalion, now bogged on the beach north of it. His platoon peeling off the company to fight an entire panzer division alone and feeling a lot like the Three Hundred Spartans must have.

It reminded him of more recent history as well, when the relief force advanced to its doom against the Axis defenses around Sidi bou Zid. Only this time Wade was in one of the tanks, and instead of a battalion, they were a single measly platoon.

Göring's finest was going to run right over him.

Only a stroke of luck would save him now. He prayed Dog would throw a track or break down, or that Russo would come to his senses, turn his big boy around, and drive in the opposite direction.

The man wouldn't, which was why he made a better commander than Wade, who was too rational for the job. Being a commander meant following orders even if they were irrational and likely to get you killed.

"We're almost off the beach," Russo said, sounding satisfied.

Wade exchanged a glance with Swanson, who shook his head.

"Fire, here we come," the loader said. "Hey, New Guy."

"What?" Payne said from the bog station.

"You're about to pop your cherry and get your ass kicked at the same time."

"Leave the guy alone," Wade said. "Anybody with eyes can see this is a fool's mission."

"Another thousand yards," Russo said, "and we'll be on the Biazzo Ridge, ready to swing west and kick Göring's clunkers in the nuts."

Swanson rolled his eyes toward their commander. "Except for fools. But that's the Army, ain't it? Send the stupid to do what can't be done."

Torn between wanting to run like hell and rush forward to get it over with, Wade returned to his scope. Getting blown up in Sicily would solve at least one of his problems: what to do about Alice.

While aboard the LST, he'd finally opened and read her letter. She hadn't even known he'd enlisted until Larry Enfield sent her a cable from Tunisia letting her know he was wounded in action. She wanted Wade to know she was sorry and beside herself with worry about him. She understood if he wanted a divorce, but she hoped he wouldn't leave her.

Alice still loved him, and she wanted him home.

He'd lost her photo when Boomer burned up in Tunisia. The memory of her face had faded. Wade was coming to understand the brain was unreliable. It forgot what shouldn't be forgotten, made impulsive decisions like joining the Army in the middle of the bloodiest war in human history, and gave itself sound and practical advice it promptly ignored.

The heart, however, never forgot, and it was always true.

Even now, strapped in and on his way to face the very high probability of his death, he ached for her. His brain warned him he'd possibly never be able to trust her again, told him he was young and there were plenty of fish. Despite its wounds, his heart didn't care. From the day Wade had gone to sea, his heart had steadily, hour by hour, worn down his will.

Like Russo, he'd obey an irrational order and rush to his doom. If he survived today, which appeared unlikely.

"Men, in case we get bopped today," Ackley buzzed over the interphone, "I just want you all to know you're a bunch of grade-A jerks."

The crew erupted into laughter.

"Seriously, if I get killed, it'll be a relief, because you're all so stupid."

"Nobody's getting killed today," Russo said. "I'm not, anyway."

"Sicilian Superman!" Wade crowed.

"Bomb, ba bomb!" Payne sang.

"I envy you your attitude, Tony."

Outside the tank, the Destroyers cheered.

"Destroyers 2, this is Destroyers 2 Actual," Lieutenant Pierce said over the radio. "We're un-assing this beach. Follow on my Delilah, and standby for further orders. Out."

Wade leaned into his scope. The ground rose into the Piano Lupo highland, which was lost in palms and colorful oleander. The objective was a strategic junction of roads northwest toward Gela. If the Germans captured it and placed tanks on it, they'd be in range to rain hell across the entire beach.

Second Platoon was tasked to race there and hold it. The five tanks would roll up onto the Biazzo Ridge until it reached Highway 115 and swing west across the Dirillo Bridge over the Acate River.

Clearing the trees, the platoon plunged into a rolling valley before mounting another hill surrounded by burned-out wheat fields covered in smoldering stubble. Heat radiated from the scorched soil. Convection currents and Delilah's tracks churned clouds of ash that blew across Wade's scope. He sweated as the warming turret steadily cooked the tankers.

The clang of panzer fire grew louder by the moment.

"We aren't getting to Piano Lupo," Wade said. "They're here already."

"Destroyers 2, this is Destroyers 2 Actual. The road ahead is the coastal highway. Clock nine, follow on my Delilah."

"Driver, you heard the man," Russo said. "Drive to the sound of the guns!"

Wade wiped a fresh wave of sweat from his forehead. "Oh, brother."

The ash cloud cleared as Dog heaved its thirty-ton bulk onto the road and swung into Delilah's wake, building speed on smooth, solid ground. The roar of Dog's big aviation engine filled the turret. A mile from the sea, Highway 115 snaked through the wrinkled and humped landscape, offering glimpses of a terrific battle at Dirillo Bridge. Smoke and dust hung over the area, through which Messerschmitts dove in strafing runs. Tons of earth exploded into the air from tank and artillery blasts.

The column hurtled toward this nightmare.

"Lord," Swanson muttered at his periscope. "If it ain't bedbugs, it's ants."

Facing it, Wade decided, if he lived through this, he'd take Alice back. She'd strayed in a moment of weakness, and it had broken his heart. But a broken heart was nothing. A broken heart healed. A broken heart didn't snap bones and rupture organs and burn you to a crisp in screaming agony. It was cake compared to a German AP shell turning your turret into a meat grinder.

I'll take you back, Alice, he thought in rising panic. *I'll love you, and we'll buy a house and have babies and raise them, and then we'll grow old together.*

"Are we loaded?" he yelled. "When are we loading?"

"Do it," Russo ordered, rubbing the Iron Cross he wore around his neck as if for luck. "Shot."

Swanson pulled a black armor-piercing round from the ready rack and wiped it with a rag. Then he kissed it for luck and shoved it into the breech.

Wade jumped at the loader's shoulder tap.

"You're up, Prof," Swanson said. "You'd better shoot straight."

"I'll do it but only because you threatened me,"

Wade growled.

"That's right," Swanson coaxed. "Let it out."

"You want to see me shoot straight? Join the German Army!"

The loader laughed. "'Theirs not to reason why, theirs but to do and die: Into the valley of death rode the six hundred!' They're salutin' the angels now!"

"Contact!" Russo called out. "Button up! That goes for your big mouth too, Animal. Stay sharp!"

"Get in line on my three!" Pierce shouted over the radio. "Pick your targets, and fire when I give the order. We're right on the bastards' flank!"

Ackley maneuvered Dog on Delilah's right, giving Wade a clear view of the battle raging at Dirillo Bridge. Panzers struggled through an olive grove on the right. More rolled among the hills around the bridge, taking on American infantry who'd strong-pointed the intersection in concrete pillboxes captured from Italian coastal defense forces. The panzers blazed away at them at close range.

Far out on the other side of the river, additional German armor had crossed the Gela Plain and reached the highway to drop rounds on the beach and approaching landing craft. That meant they'd already smashed through the infantry regiment standing in their way.

The only thing stopping them now from driving straight to the sea was a ragged line of cooks and yeomen down on the sand dunes.

Hang tight, Wade thought. *The cavalry is coming...*

"Get ready to throw Jerry a surprise party," Russo

said. "Gunner, tank at one o'clock, shot, one-one hundred."

Slick with sweat now, Wade zeroed his reticle on the rear turret of a dusty Mark IV painted in a gray camouflage pattern.

Once, aiming a 75 at another human being had filled him with an unsettling guilt, but no longer. He wanted nothing more than to obliterate these guys.

"Stand by," Russo said.

The tanks thundered line abreast across a wheat field.

Russo: "Range, nine hundred now. Stand by for the order!"

"Come on." Wade nudged the elevation wheel to adjust for the shortening range. "Come on, come on, come on."

The enemy tank turned left, exposing eight wheels and confirming it as a Mark IV, and it rolled forward. Another tank lumbered into his view.

"Tiger at two o'clock!" he cried.

"Stay on the Mark IV! Eight hundred!"

The Tiger's front plate was painted with a broad, red grin filled with shark teeth. It seemed the Germans had their own artists in their armored forces.

"They're going to see us any second," Swanson shouted. "What the hell are you waiting for?"

Russo shouted back, "The order, *scustumad*."

"Shoot now!"

"Shut up—"

The radio buzzed: "All Destroyers 2, stop!"

Ackley yanked the sticks before Russo could give

the order.

Pierce: "Fire!"

"Fire!" Russo cried.

Wade mashed the floor pedal. "On the way!"

Dog bucked as it hurled the AP shell at the Mark IV and blew a hole in its weak rear armor. A tongue of blue flame and sparks flared from it as the panzer ground to a halt.

"Yes!" Wade screamed. "Yes! Yes!"

The Mark IV was burning. Beyond, another panzer had been hit in the platoon's first volley. Caught flat-footed, the Germans hadn't begun reacting yet.

"Gunner, traverse right! Tiger, shot, seven-five-zero, lead three mils, fire!"

Wade feverishly worked his controls. "On the way!"

The scope filled with blurred white shot as the platoon opened up on the milling panzers with another volley. He missed the Tiger, whose turret was now slowly turning toward the American armor.

"Up two, fire!"

Wade stomped the pedal. "On the way!"

The shot pounded the Tiger's flank and blew out one of its sprocket wheels. Still alive, the monstrous panzer jerked to the side as it fired back with a flash and puff of smoke. The round blurred past Wade's scope. Near miss!

The hot shell casing banged on the turret floor. The acrid tang of burnt gunpowder stung his nostrils.

"He's immobilized!" Russo gloated. "Loader, HE! Gunner, up a hair! Fire!"

Swanson shoved a high-explosive round into the

breech. "Up!"

"On the way!"

The next shell smashed the Tiger's turret with a heart-stopping explosion. The concussion threw dust off the metal monster's armor.

"Again, fire!"

"On the way!"

Even with repeated hits, the shells didn't penetrate the big tank's armor, but every hit rattled the tank's crew and had a probability of damaging its systems.

"Hit him with WP!" Russo said. "Smoke them!"

"On the way!"

The white phosphorous round blasted a blazing patch across the turret and shrouded it in a blooming cloud of thick, white smoke.

"Load AP! Driver, get me close for a kill shot!"

"I see them!" Payne called out. "The crew's running!"

Believing their Tiger to be on fire, the German tankers were making a run for it. To his credit, Payne shot at them with the bow machine gun, but showed a novice's aversion to shooting people in the back by firing over their heads.

"Shoot the Germans," Wade yelled.

Payne adjusted his aim but still kept missing.

Wade tweaked the gun and lobbed the HE round while opening up with his coaxial machine gun. The black-uniformed tankers went down.

"Kill all Nazis," he said into the interphone. "Tony, I need a target!"

"No targets," Russo said.

Wade scanned the battlefield, but nothing moved

among the burning panzer wrecks. Then he spotted the tail end of a Mark IV disappearing into a series of olive groves.

"They're retreating," he said. "I can't believe we—"

The air trembled with a chorus of ghostly howls that chilled him to the bone. Five- and six-inch shells passing overhead.

The olive groves erupted in a withering chain of explosions.

"Well, all right," Ackley said.

The U.S. Navy was firing everything they had at the Germans. Hundreds of shells fell along the entire front, smashing vehicles and infantry and shaking the earth. The pounding went on until nearly every tree had been flattened to expose the shattered hulks of panzers among a burning and cratered landscape.

The survivors scuttled away until they dropped out of sight. Only plumes of smoke rising from dozens of burning tanks in the distant wheat fields evidenced the Germans were ever here.

The men sat in stunned silence as the firing faded and the only sounds the tankers heard were their idling engine and the ringing in their ears.

"Where you going, Jerry?" Sergeant Cranston said over the radio, which filled with laughter, whoops, and taunts.

Wade counted nine enemy tanks knocked out between the flanking attack and another seven destroyed by the Navy's big guns. "Wow."

They'd survived. More than that, they'd won. And the Americans hadn't lost a single tank in the attack.

"Wow," he said again.

Russo was shouting outside.

Wade frowned at Swanson. "What's he doing?"

"He's standing on the turret, pounding his chest, and yelling at the Krauts like the crazy, little, ginzo runt he is."

"See what you get when you fuck with me, Jerry?" Russo howled. "I killed your Tiger! That's what you get! You get dead!"

Swanson laughed. Wade joined in, his own laughter edged with hysteria, the laughter of a man who'd escaped the gallows, the laughter of the mad.

The loader stopped and sneered at him. "What's this? We're friends now?"

"Yeah," Wade sneered back. "You're my best and only friend."

This only made Swanson laugh again. "There's hope for you yet, Professor."

Like the Three Hundred Spartans, the platoon had prevailed with a little help from the gods—that is, the U.S. Navy. Wade wondered if the Spartan heroes got on each other's nerves too. He decided they probably did.

CHAPTER EIGHT

THE TIGER

Corporal Swanson's laughter faded to a chuckle. "Nice one, Professor. Maybe we are friends. Who can say? But you forgot one important thing."

"Oh, brother," Wade said, all weariness now. He was already tiring of their game, which was his problem; the man had no stamina. "What?"

"On the way!" Swanson tilted in his seat and pumped out an explosive fart.

"Goddamn it, Animal!"

Swanson opened his hatch to breathe fresh air and take in the view. His jaw dropped as his eyes swept the shattered landscape. "Lord. If it weren't a shithole before, it surely is now."

The Navy's big guns had turned the Sicilian countryside into a landscape resembling the moon. Under a vast pall of smoke and dust, smoking craters and flaming vehicles dotted the hills as far as the eye could see. The shelling had set more of the wheat fields ablaze around smashed barns and peasant homes. Navy spotting planes circled overhead in the murk.

Russo stood on the turret, panting and thumping his chest. "We did it."

"We're alive, *Duce*." Swanson leaned to light the tip of a Chesterfield. "I count that as one for the win column."

"We're alive," the commander echoed dully, skeptically. Then he sagged as exhaustion overtook him.

"Thank the Lord for the Navy is all I got to say. They saved the day."

"We did our part too." Russo gazed down from the ridge toward the American beachhead. "Still a real mess down there, but they're safe now."

Swanson took in the jumble of men, vehicles, and scattered gear. "It's like a traffic jam and train crash had a baby." A thought struck him. "It's really something..."

"What's that?"

"How we always get punched in the face fifty times and somehow win."

Russo lowered himself into the cupola. "The lieutenant wants us to meet up with the paratroopers those Tigers were pounding. Driver, move out."

"All right," Ackley said as if the order were a nag.

Dog rolled with the rest of the platoon to the bridge, where fighters with the 505th Parachute Infantry Regiment flagged them down. These hard men had dropped out of the night sky onto Sicily to capture the ridge and hold it against impossible odds. Swanson smiled at the idea of these elite warriors giving him a hero's welcome for knocking out the panzers that had been stomping them.

"Where the hell were you, you fucking tankers?" An airborne rifleman glowered at Swanson, the nearest target of his wrath. "We've been screaming for armor support all day. Some of the best men I've ever known are dead now."

Swanson flicked his cigarette into the dirt. "Too bad for them."

"You son of a..." The soldier dropped his rifle and lunged forward, but his comrades grabbed hold of him. "Son of a bitch!"

A red-faced sergeant glared up at Swanson. "What's the matter with you?"

"I'm a loader," Swanson said. "I go where they send me, when they send me. You want me to say sorry your guys got killed?" He spat. "Ain't my fault."

Russo shook his head. "*Mannaggia*, Animal, they were fighting Tigers with bazookas. Have a little heart."

"Ain't my fault," Swanson said again. "And if you know anything about me, *Duce*, it's I ain't big in the heart department. If they want to take it out on somebody who actually did this, they should have grabbed a prisoner."

"Our own fucking fleet tried to shoot us down, and now this," the paratrooper raged, on the verge of tears. "It's every man for himself."

These words shook Swanson. The soldier was borrowing his line that, beneath all the brothers-in-arms crap, it really was every man out for himself. But that was the thing: It was *his* line. Hearing a good man like this—you had to be a special kind of brave or dumb to volunteer for the airborne—say it was heartbreaking. And Swanson didn't even really believe it himself, not after what his crew had gone through together in Tunisia. Yes, saying they were all brothers was the worst kind of crap, but so was saying they weren't.

"If we could have gotten here sooner, we would," Russo told the sergeant. "We didn't get landed until this morning. Then we got bogged on the beach—"

"Mac, shut up." Swanson dropped into the turret and re-emerged with a bottle of cheap gin he'd scrounged in Algiers. "Hey, Sarge." He extended it toward the airborne sergeant. "We go where they send us, when they send us."

The sergeant took the bottle. "All right."

"Sorry about your guys. No hard feelings."

Without waiting for a reply, the loader stepped off the turret onto the rear deck and hopped to the ground.

"Where are you going?" Russo called after him.

Swanson ignored him and started walking. He wanted to see the devil close up.

The dense phosphorous smoke had almost dissipated on the easterly sea breeze, revealing the scorched and scarred turret with its open hatches. The wide track sagged in a crumpled mess around the eight large wheels. The acrid stink of motor oil and garlic smell of white phosphor hung in the air.

Up close, the tank was a beast, menacing even immobilized. Swanson guessed it had to weigh at least twice as much as Dog. The thick, welded armor plate, the interleaved and overlapping wheels mounted on twin torsion bars, the massive and deadly 88 gun. The good mobility despite its weight. He had a gearhead's eye and whistled at the craftsmanship.

"It's beautiful." Payne snapped a picture.

The rest of the crew had joined him to take a closer look at the monster that haunted their nightmares. The bog touched the thick armor and flinched. Scored by the HE rounds, the metal was black and still hot from the white phosphorous shell.

"I'd rather be in one than fight it," Ackley said.

"The Army won't ever give us one," Swanson said. "Not when they can throw a lot of M4s into the fight. We're as disposable as them airborne guys."

"You guys have it all wrong," Wade countered. "We can't make tanks like this. It's too heavy for most bridges. If it breaks down on one of these narrow roads, how do you get it off? Its size makes it easy pickings for planes. As far as us building them, how do you even get it on a ship?"

"I'd rather be in one than fight it," Ackley repeated.

"We did fight it," Russo said. "And we killed it."

"Because we got the drop on him," Wade said. "If it had been the other way around, one shot would have been the end of us."

"Thanks for the usual cheerful outlook, Professor," Swanson said. "What I want to know is what else they're working on. The Krauts are good at this."

Before anybody could speculate, Lieutenant Pierce returned from meeting with the airborne commander and mounted his tank. "Let's go, Destroyers. We've got an airfield to take!"

"But I didn't get a souvenir," Ackley complained.

"Why?" Swanson said. "You think you're gonna make it home?"

"Now who's being cheerful?" the kid muttered. "Fun-killer."

"Animal's the original fun-killer, Ack-Ack," Wade

said. "You'll never be as good at fun-killing as him."

The tankers returned to Dog, mounted up, and plugged in.

"Driver, crank the engine," Russo ordered and added to Swanson, "That was a nice thing you did giving those airborne guys some hooch."

"They earned it." Swanson didn't want to talk about it.

"And you said you weren't big in the heart department."

He scowled. "Don't go thinking you know me, Mac. I ain't one thing or the other, and I ain't gonna pour sugar just to make somebody feel better, especially the likes of you."

"I think the real you is coming out," Russo said. "But you've been an asshole so long you think being a better man makes you weak."

"If that's true, then you're the best man I know."

Russo opened his yap but seemed to think better of it and shrugged instead. "Driver, start the engine. Move out, and follow on Delilah."

"All right," said Ackley.

The tanks crossed the Acate River and rolled toward Gela.

"Hey, Sergeant," Payne said. "Tell us something about the town's history."

"Why would you want to know?" Swanson muttered. "You're as bad as Eight Ball, New Guy."

"Gela was founded by the Greeks and was a major player in Sicily," the Professor pronounced, adopting his lecture tone. "One of its biggest claims to fame was

Aeschylus lived and died here."

"Who was that?" Russo said, throwing gasoline on the fire.

"He's considered the inventor of the trilogy and the father of tragedy. A tragedy being a play where a character has a reversal of fortune, usually for the worst. The audience suffers along with the character, which can also involve catharsis, as often they can see what's coming."

"Just like us," Swanson said.

"It definitely sounds like Gela," Russo said. "The town where tragedy was born is looking pretty tragic itself."

Swanson opened his hatch to take a look. After an hour's drive along the coastal highway, Dog rolled onto the town's cobblestone streets and waded into a jam of people and vehicles. The Army pamphlet said around thirty thousand people lived here, though the war had shaved that total. One out of ten of the gray, tile-roofed houses was in ruins, the result of shelling from both American ships and German artillery.

Colorful gladioli decorated the windows of the houses that still stood. From arched doorways, children stared in fascination and fear. The air stank of fish and gunpowder and heaps of corpses being hauled toward the beach in creaking, mule-drawn carts. Keening Sicilian women trailed after them.

A column of dazed prisoners jogged past. Among them, Army rangers—just as hard as the airborne and twice as crazy, if that was possible—milled around with haggard, sooty faces, shrugging off local peddlers trying to sell them lemons.

Swanson said, "Well, Mac, I guess you would call that, what do you call it, when something looks like the opposite of what you'd expect—"

"Ironic," Wade chirped over the interphone.

"You sure about that?" He didn't see what it had to do with iron.

"Yes."

"I'll take your word for—"

"*Vinni la primavera, li mennuli sù n'ciuri,*" Russo sang in a rich tenor voice.

"What the hell, Mac?"

The commander swept his arms as he sang, his eyes fixed on a buxom Sicilian girl carrying a bundle of firewood perched on her head. Her wide hips swished as she balanced her load with careful steps. Despite the Battle of Gela, these people had daily chores they needed to tend to, and Russo was still on his quest for the perfect dame to be his wife.

"*Lu focu di l'ammuri,*" he crowed. "*Lu cori m'addurmò!*"

"*Viva* America," the woman said, her eyes pure venom.

"*M'av'a scusari!*" Swanson called out to her.

Her mouth dropped open in astonishment. The tank rolled past. Next in line, Dealer's crew whistled as they passed the woman.

"What was that about?" Swanson said. "You singing?"

"It's a folk song about love in spring."

"And she didn't jump at the chance of you courting

her. Lord, you'd think after blowing up her town and probably killing half her family, she'd be all over you."

"When you said, *I'm sorry* to her, she looked genuinely touched. And you said you weren't big in the heart department."

"I should have known that pickup line you gave me was bull."

The commander breathed deep. "You smell that?"

"I smell dead fish and chicken shit."

"It's crushed fennel." Russo beamed at the battered town of shell-shocked people. "I feel like I'm home."

Dog passed a building Swanson guessed was the local fascist headquarters, its walls pockmarked by small arms fire and bearing a graffitied slogan Russo translated as, *Mussolini defends the nation*. Under it, a soldier had chalked the words, *Benito is finito*. A ragged American flag nailed to the wall declared the building to be under new ownership. More rangers loitered, laughing at the tanks and giving them the finger. *Just like doughs*, Swanson thought. They got mad when you showed up and drew shellfire, and they got mad when they needed tank support and you didn't appear in a flash like a genie to grant their wish.

"Destroyers 2, this is Destroyers 2 Actual," the radio blared. "Keep moving through the town. We're rejoining the company on the west side. Out."

"Drive on, Ack-Ack," Russo said.

The platoon broke free of the crowds and left Gela. Passing abandoned pillboxes and crushed lengths of barbed wire, the tanks drove onto wheat fields ravaged by shelling. The rest of the company waited here in a peach orchard among the entire battalion. Swanson smirked, expecting a hero's welcome for the mighty platoon that stopped the German counterattack in its tracks.

"Thought you were dead," a tanker called out to him.

The rest looked rankled. In fact, not a single man looked happy. Then the stink hit him.

Beyond the tank park, the fields were covered in dead. Italian infantrymen in blue uniforms lay scattered among the craters, some half buried in soil, others naked, still more ripped to shreds, all of them sightless and staring and surrounded by clouds of black flies. White phosphorous had reduced swathes of them to a charred paste. Some had even been blasted into the trees and hung from the branches. The shattered wrecks of Renault and Fiat tanks lay strewn across this slaughterhouse.

It was here the vaunted Livorno Division had marched in neat columns against the rangers dug in west of Gela, only to be brutally mauled on open ground by mortars and the Navy's big guns.

Russo turned pale at the sight of it, and Swanson didn't feel so good himself. There were thousands of them. A single bombardment had devastated an entire division of Italy's best infantry.

"God almighty," the loader said as Dog slowed to a halt.

"It's like something out of the Old Testament," Russo breathed.

Swanson nodded. These guys were the enemy and

had been coming to kill him, and good riddance to the bastards. At the same time, it was hard not to feel a little bit sorry for them. There was something personal about it; two men went into a room, and only one came out alive. It was satisfying to be the survivor but also unsettling.

At times like these, he remembered this was a war between human beings, not nations. Under the uniform, they all lived and died the same. The war didn't care who it killed. It could just as easily have been him.

If these tankers were his brothers, then so were the airborne. If the airborne were his brothers, then so were these Italians.

He shoved aside these feelings and then stomped them with his boot for good measure. If he intended to survive this war with his head as well as his body intact, he would have to forget these men were human beings.

And after the fighting was done, he could try to forget all of it.

"We're staying here an hour to wait for the armored infantry," Russo said. "Then we're moving north to take Ponte Olivo Airfield."

"I'm gonna pick some of them peaches before everybody else gets them all," Ackley said.

Russo's eyes were haunted. "You do that, Ack-Ack."

"Me, I'm gonna have a drink," Swanson said.

Before the commander could protest, he lowered himself into the turret and found another bottle of gin.

A moment later, Russo dropped inside to join him for a belt.

CHAPTER NINE

THE AIRFIELD

Sweating in bright Sicilian sunlight, Corporal Russo ate his can of dull beef and vegetable stew and washed it down with swallows from his canteen. Behind him, most of the dead Livorno Division rotted where they lay while prisoners dragged bodies into mass graves marked with a simple *ED*, which stood for *enemy dead*.

When he finished his chow, he started to get up to help with Dog's maintenance. Bogie wheels needed greasing, the gas tank had to be filled, optical sights required adjusting. Oh, and the track needed tightening, batteries and fluids had to be checked, and the ready rack had to be restocked from their ammo storage. The other crewmen were already at it with their wrenches and grease guns.

Instead of helping, however, he sat back down on the turret and reached for the bottle of gin. Driving through Gela had felt like a homecoming. The sights and smells of the town had triggered some ancestral memory. If Mussolini hadn't driven out his family, he'd be living east of here, near Syracuse, which was only about sixty miles away. If Mussolini hadn't formed his Pact of Steel with Hitler, he wouldn't have come here to fight.

It gave him vertigo, like he was a traitor invading

his own home. Then he reminded himself he wasn't invading it; he was liberating it from a tyrant. His ancestral countrymen might not know it yet from all the bombs falling on their homes, but he was a hero.

Either way, Russo felt better knowing he hadn't shot any Italians today. Germans, he didn't mind killing at all. In his mind, they were the true invaders, an occupation army forcing Italy into a war it could no longer afford.

Mickey Cranston walked up and leaned against Dog. "How's she running?"

"Like a top," Russo said, feeling a little boozy. "No problems. You?"

"Blew a bogie wheel riding through Gela, but we got her fixed up. The transmission's getting fussy, though. I..."

"What's up?"

The tank sergeant cupped his hands to light one of his foul-smelling cigars. "I was just wondering if it was always like that. Combat."

Russo scoffed. "Hell no. Compared to Tunisia, that was easy. We got lit up there. We only got the drop on the Krauts once."

"I saw you pound that Tiger until it didn't know if it was coming or going."

"I would have gotten out and punched it in the gearbox if I thought it'd do some good. You see one of those things, you throw everything you've got at it."

"Yeah," Cranston said. "We scratched one too. A Mark IV. Punched a hole in its ass. We could hear the crew screaming as it started burning, clear as day." The man paled. "Then some of its ammo cooked off and put an end to that."

"You did good, Mickey. It was him or you."

"Right. It could have been me."

Russo understood the killing bothered the man but not nearly as much as the idea of being killed himself. Of burning alive.

Russo handed him the bottle.

Cranston took a drink while he gazed across the killing fields. "You aren't scared, are you? Because you're a veteran. You've already seen worse, huh?"

"I'm not scared because I'm not," Russo said. "I've made it this far, I figure I can make it a while longer. Today, I killed a Tiger. I'm going to shoot anything they throw at me. Nothing's going to stop me going home."

Captain Ratliff and Lieutenant Pierce strode among the tanks. The captain's icy blue stare settled on Cranston. "We're moving out in ten minutes. Stow that booze now, and don't let me see it again."

"Yes, sir." The tank sergeant took another quick swig and handed the bottle back to Russo. "What's the word, Captain?"

Ratliff waited for the rest of the platoon's tank commanders to gather around. "Lieutenant Pierce told me what you hotshots did at Biazzo Ridge, getting fire baptized. That was shit hot tank work."

Beside him, Pierce beamed at the praise.

"By the time the rest of us got off the beach, it was over," Ratliff said.

"You made good time all the same," said Butch, who commanded Dealer.

"Yeah, well, we had your logs, and the engineers

blew a path for us through the dunes." The captain shot Payne a withering look. "With bangalores."

Payne wisely said nothing.

"One more good fight," Ratliff went on. "We take Ponte Olivo, we'll have a base for our birds to take on all these Kraut planes we've got raining bombs on us. Word is the Hermann Göring Division is un-assing to the north and east. After we take the airfield, we'll have a clear path to Messina. We take Messina, we're done with this shithole."

The tankers smiled. Put like that, their survival chances looked pretty good, and victory would make all the hardship worth it.

"Then let's go take an airfield, Captain," said Butter, Democracy's commander.

"Drive on, Sergeant. That's the aggressive spirit I want to see."

Cranston said, "Sir, we used up a good amount of ordnance on the ridge. About twenty percent of our load. Any word on resupply?"

"The landing zones are still a mess. Your restock is a needle in that haystack. Beg, borrow, and steal from the rest of the company. Make do."

"Sir?" Russo said. "Any idea what we're going up against?"

"The Heinies aren't going to give up their airfield easily, and there are still plenty of Italians around," Ratliff said. "With the ginzos, it's a coin toss whether they're going to give up at the first shot or fight like wild animals."

The captain pointed at the killing fields west of

them. "It's all the same to me. They put up a fight, they'll end up like their dead friends here. We didn't bring our big boys all this way to mess around. This is our island now. Get ready to move out. Dismissed."

The tankers cracked grins as they returned to their vehicles, finished whatever maintenance and scrounging they needed to do, and mounted up for the assault. Hugging an armful of freshly picked peaches, Ackley ran back to the tank as the order came to crank up and start the engines. With a grief-stricken expression, Payne gazed at the field of dead for a while longer, then turned with his hands in his pockets and mounted his station.

As far as Russo was concerned, the battle plan was simple: support the Big Red One's assault on Ponte Olivo Airfield. Advance to contact, and blow up anything that got in the way. Wait for the rest of the regiment, and advance on Messina. Other than that, he'd do whatever the platoon commander told him.

He stood in the cupola and felt the four-hundred-horsepower engine's energy surge through the tank's armor and into his heart. He shed all thoughts of the mounds of dead and any nagging doubts about immortality. On the big chessboard, he was a rook, sometimes a knight. In his little domain, though, he was king, acting through four other men operating a thirty-ton dragon.

As much as he missed driving, the view was so much better up here.

"Destroyers 2, this is Destroyers 2 Actual," Lieutenant Pierce said over the radio, still jovial from the praise he'd gotten from Captain Ratliff. "Our company will be the lead element."

Laden with gear like a traveling caravan, Destroyer Company uncoiled and drove toward the road. A swarm of tanks, trucks, halftracks, and mobile artillery followed in its dust. They crushed the oleander and columned onto Highway 117, which would bring them to the airfield six miles distant.

Cranston's singing filled the radio. "I'm glad I came, but I'm ready to go. Give it back to the ginzos, I'm anxious to blow!"

The radio filled with laughter.

Russo scowled. *Ginzos, dagos, guineas, wops.* Always this shit.

Dog started balking.

"Driver, pull off right and stop so we can look at the engine."

"The engine's fine," Ackley said. "It's my belly. It's killing me. I can't keep my hands on the sticks." The tank balked again. "*Ow.*"

"I told you not to eat all those peaches," Wade said.

"You better not shit in my tank," Swanson growled.

"Pull off the road, driver." Russo keyed his radio. "Destroyers 2 Actual, this is Destroyers 2-5. We're stopping to swap drivers."

"Acknowledged, 2-5. Make it quick, we're on the clock."

"Roger."

Dog parked on the side of the highway. Ackley jumped out of his station clutching his guts and scrambled to squat in a clump of jasmine.

"Take his spot, Payne," Russo said.

"It's been a while since Fort Knox, Corporal."

"Just do it, *gidrul*."

"Sure. Roger."

Wade chuckled. "How many did he eat?"

Russo turned to see the armored force's main body catching up. "Coming or staying, Ackley! We're moving out."

The skinny kid stumbled out of the bushes pulling his trousers up and trailing a stream of toilet paper behind him. "All right!"

"*Maronna mia*," Russo muttered. "All right, he's in. Driver, move out."

Dog's transmission made a grinding noise and bucked at Payne's novice shifting. Then it jerked onto the road before settling into a steady march.

"Put Dog in high gear, and step on it. We need to catch up." Russo glared at the back of Ackley's helmeted head. "Ack-Ack, what the hell are you doing?"

The kid slurped into the interphone. "Eating a peach."

He sighed but put it aside. Everything was still going well. Dog was at the rear of the company now but still in the game. They were driving on a good road, and Sicily was turning out to be far less dusty than Africa was.

"Destroyers 2, this is Destroyers 2 Actual," the radio intoned. "We're rolling through the 26th Infantry Regiment's turf now. We'll be stopping to let them ride with us. Maintain dispersion."

"Driver, you heard the man," Russo said. "Keep a

thirty-yard distance. Stop when the big boy in front of us stops. Friendly doughs will be mounting Dog."

"Hey, Swanson," Ackley said, smacking his lips. "Ain't that what you hillbillies do when you get bored?"

Russo didn't need the interphone to hear the resulting hilarity.

"Actually, Peaches," the loader said in a menacing tone, "we throw pipsqueaks out of moving vehicles while they shit themselves."

"Speaking of which," Ackley said, "I don't feel so good again."

"Too bad," Russo snarled. "Hold it, you *mariul*."

The column stopped as infantry emerged from the honeysuckle on both sides of the road. A squad climbed onto Dog and settled around the turret and sponsons.

"About time," the sergeant said as he got comfortable. "You tankers are never around when we want you and always show up when we don't need you."

"We go where they send us, when they send us," Russo said, quoting Swanson. "Anything else is above my pay grade."

"Fair enough. At least you're here now. The name's Durante."

"Any relation to the performer?"

"Nope," the sergeant said. "Not that I'm aware, anyway."

"'Inka dinka doo,'" Russo rasped in Jimmy Durante's signature accent. "What a guy. I'm Russo. It's good to meet a *paesan*."

Durante's handsome face scowled under his dirty helmet. "I always wanted to go see the Old Country.

Not like this, though, huh?"

"I hear you."

The column crossed the coastal plain, passing wheat and barley fields, vineyards, and orchards. Several miles out from Ponte Olivo, the ground sloped down toward the airfield, which lay against a backdrop of rocky hills.

"This is where we get off," Durante said. "See you around, Russo."

"Good luck, *paesan*."

The tanks deployed in a line across the wheat fields. Squads of doughs clumped behind their cover in grape formations. Trucks unloaded the armored infantry, and the men formed columns behind the tanks.

"Hey," Wade said. "Do you guys see that castle on the hill over there?"

Russo raised his binoculars. A boxy stone keep stood on one of the scrubby hills overlooking the airfield. It was probably occupied by Axis guns. Once the Americans captured the high ground, they'd be able to use it as a springboard to leap to Messina.

"Norman," Wade said. "A motte-and-bailey design. The motte is a raised earthwork surrounded by the bailey, a fortified enclosure. They were very common in medieval—"

"Advance to contact," Pierce said over the radio.

"—Europe, as they were cheap and easy—"

"Not now, Wade," Russo cut him off. "Driver, move out. Button up!"

Line abreast across a mile of ground, the company rumbled toward the airfield.

"They can see us coming and will try to get as many

of their planes in the air as they can," the lieutenant added. "I spotted at least four 88s that are going to try to stop us. Don't halt unless you're shooting. We're taking that airfield now."

The radio filled with whoops from the other commanders.

Trailed by their infantry columns, the tanks advanced at a steady speed. Puffs of smoke appeared from the airfield and the hills beyond. The German 88s opened fire in green blurs that tore through the air. Russo glanced at Cranston who flinched in his cupola.

Dirt rained across the tank from a nearby explosion.

Sizing up his target, Russo rattled off instructions. "Gunner, antitank, eleven o'clock, HE, traverse left, steady, steady..."

Swanson loaded the HE round. "You're up!"

A tank exploded with a bang that rent the atmosphere. Pieces of metal thudded and clanged across the field.

Across the line, the Destroyers ground to a halt and fired back.

"On!" Russo cried. "Fire!"

"On the way!"

Dog shuddered as the tank spat a high-velocity HE shell at the 88. Russo observed the effect with his binoculars.

"Short," he said. "Right ten, up eight."

His range changes were in mils. Each mil equaled fifty yards. When shooting at a target more than a thousand yards away, a tank had to bracket its target. An inexperienced tank commander often made range changes that were too small. Called creeping, this wasted time and ammo.

Bracketing the right way involved overcorrecting to straddle the target. The longer the range, the bigger the corrections. Then the commander halved until he had the target good and zeroed.

"Fire!"

"On the way!"

The next round flashed behind the 88. "Over! Down four mils, fire!"

"On the way!"

The round fell a little short. Additional bursts around the 88 indicated other tanks were firing at the same gun. The radio filled with shouting men as Pierce struggled to coordinate their fire.

A shell ricocheted off a nearby tank with a piercing metallic shriek.

"Up two, fire!"

"On the way!"

Dog's shell smashed the ground beside the 88, shredding its crew and knocking it off its mounting. The heavy gun toppled in a cloud of dust.

"Hit! We got him!"

"Give me a target, Tony," Wade shouted back. "I don't see any."

Russo scanned the airbase with his binoculars. "We got them all except the ones in the hills, which are covered by a smokescreen."

"Good," the gunner said, more in relief than celebration.

"Driver, move out!"

The tanks lumbered down the slope toward the airfield. The infantry swarmed out from behind to take it by assault and ran into heavy rifle and machine gun fire. The tanks raked these positions then advanced to lay waste to the hangars and planes parked along the airstrip. Point-blank HE rounds shredded the German fighters and dive-bombers where they stood. A plane lunged into the air only to lose a wing and splash back to earth. Bolting airmen crumpled under withering machine gun fire.

Wade stomped the pedal to blast a Messerschmitt into flaming wreckage.

Between the infantry and the tanks, the German resistance ebbed. From the cockpits of the shattered Luftwaffe planes, snipers shot at the doughs until another flurry of HE rounds pounded them into eternity.

The Destroyers shifted to aim their fire at the hills, where German infantry and more antitank guns had dug in to cover the withdrawal of the 15th Panzergrenadiers. The doughs scurried up the slopes.

Every time they killed a German, it seemed, there was another right behind him, and another behind him.

Russo didn't mind. He was here to free his homeland from the fascist yoke, and at that moment, he would have happily killed them all.

CHAPTER TEN

WHY WE FIGHT

On the airstrip, the dead lay in ragged rows, American GIs in olive drab and Germans in field gray, enemies in combat, brothers in death.

PFC Payne pondered them while he smoked a cigarette.

"Hey, New Guy," Swanson said behind him. "Gimme one of them cigs."

Payne handed one over and lit it. "What's next for us, you think?"

"If you're done staring at dead people, we need to do some maintenance."

"The commander told me to take five so he could work out a problem with Dog's powertrain. I was just thinking about the dualities in war."

The loader blew a cloud of smoke. "Dualities. Right."

"This airfield... It's ugly, but there's a strange, horrible beauty to it."

"Uh-huh."

"Humans built these amazing machines but use them to destroy each other."

"Uh-huh."

"And me too. I don't want to kill, but I want to beat the fascists. It's why I'm here. I couldn't sit back and let everybody else put their life on the line for a fight I believe in."

"Uh-huh, right," Swanson said. "Listen: I don't care. Nobody cares. You're trying to make yourself the hero of a story. You ain't a hero. There ain't no story. There's only killing and staying alive."

Payne dropped his cigarette and ground it out with his boot. "So it's all malarkey to you."

"The worst kind of malarkey. Krauts and Tommies and Eye-talians have been fighting each other forever. Why the hell is it our business?"

"Why are you even here, then?"

"Paying for my sins," the loader said. "I loved this dame, but she loved another guy, and I thought if I hurt him, she'd love me instead. The hero gets the girl, right? Wrong. Next thing I know, I'm in Sam's Circus getting shot at."

"And now you're in Sicily killing people without a real reason."

Swanson barked a bitter laugh. "I have a reason, and it's better than yours. I'm killing because, if I don't, I'll get killed." He gestured to the German dead. "Even though these bastards are just like me, I'll kill every one of them, because I ain't dying for them. And guess what, I ain't dying for you neither."

"Is that why you constantly mess with everybody? So you don't care?"

The loader glowered at him. "Here's the thing, New Guy. Next time you're on the bow gun, shoot the Nazis, or I'll make you sorry you ever joined up."

His face burning, Payne looked away. "I'll do my

part."

"You do that." Swanson snorted. "You want to put your life on the line. Well, guess what, nobody wants it. I want you to kill so I stay alive."

The war didn't give a fig about his body. It wanted his soul.

"Break time's over, Payne!" Russo called. "I need a hand here. *Sbrigati.*"

Shaken by his epiphany, Payne returned to the tank, where the commander knelt on the rear deck over the open engine bay. "Did you find the problem?"

During the fight on the airfield, the powertrain had lacked stamina. Russo had reset the ignition, topped up the coolant, and checked the water pumps, belts, water hose, and air inlet to the radiator. The culprit turned out to be a dirty fuel filter, a problem that was easily fixed with a good cleaning.

"We'll keep running down the list, just in case," Russo said. "Once we finish up, we can take Dog for a run and see how he handles."

The amount of maintenance that went into keeping Dog walking amazed Payne. A problem like a weak powertrain had fourteen possible causes. It reminded him of the proverb about how the lack of a nail cost a kingdom. *For want of a clean filter, power was lost. For want of power, a tank was lost. For want of a tank, a battle was lost. Because of a dirty filter, the war was lost.*

"What did you do before all this, Shorty?" he asked.

"Meat packing. You were a painter, right?"

"I did meat packing for a while too," Payne said. "I did a lot of things. But I was always a painter. It wasn't until just before I left that I made any money at it."

"Sounds like bad timing to me. But it's good to do what you love."

"You going back to meat packing after the war's over?"

Russo glanced at the dead lying in the sun and crossed himself. "Probably not."

"I guess it's hard to think that far ahead."

"I'm more concerned with the here and now. Speaking of which, you did all right during the fight. Driving Dog here."

"I want to do my part. I'm still finding my way, though."

"Aren't we all? Help me close the doors, and then you can give him a whirl. If Dog's running fine, maybe we can catch some shuteye like Ackley."

Payne walked around to the rear of the tank and detached the long hand crank, which he inserted into a hole in the rear hull plate. He cranked it fifty times to turn the engine over once and initiate operation.

This done, he hauled himself onto the left sponson and wiggled through the hatch into the driver's station. The interior stank of lubricating oil and old sweat. He closed the battery switch, opened the fuel shutoff valves, and placed the gearshift in neutral. After starting the engine, he drew the choke back until the engine reached a smooth hum.

"Are we going somewhere?"

Payne turned toward the voice. Sergeant Wade had been writing a letter in the gunner's seat, pouring sweat in the turret's oven heat.

"Just giving Dog a short walk. The powertrain was running weak."

"Yeah, I felt that."

"Am I bothering you?"

"No. Well, yeah. I came in here to be alone." The gunner held up his letter. "Just trying to find the right words."

"You must have wanted privacy to put up with how hot it is in here."

Russo called to him from outside. "I don't see any leaks, and he sounds good. How does he look at your end?"

Payne checked the indicators. "Looking good."

"Take him out for a quick run."

He turned to Wade. "You coming along?"

"Sure, why not."

Payne set the hand throttle and released the parking brake before shifting into second gear and releasing the clutch. This time, he didn't grind gears or let up on the clutch too fast; he was getting better at this.

The tank eased forward at two miles an hour. Russo guided him out of close quarters and onto the open field.

Payne patted the humming transmission. "Let's see what you've got, Dog."

He pressed the clutch again and shifted to third then up to the highest gear to give the tank a proper shakedown. The engine whined at the strain. Top gear wasn't ideal for off-road driving, though the field was flat and firm.

"He isn't balking," Wade yelled over the noise.

"He's running like a top." Payne downshifted and pulled on the right stick to force Dog to turn around for home.

"You should ask Tony if you can split the driving with Ack-Ack."

"Why?"

"Because Ackley doesn't have a problem shooting Germans. During the fight at the bridge, you burned through a whole belt firing over their heads."

Remembering his conversation with Swanson, Payne flushed again. The loader played the oaf but had him pegged. Payne had struggled to make sense of the war, but it was very simple. You killed, or you got yourself and your crewmates killed. These men didn't have any choice but to depend on one another with their lives. Each didn't expect anything from the other except that he could rely on him to kill so they all survived.

"I'll do what's needed," Payne said. "Whatever you guys do, I'll do."

"Not everybody's cut out for this. There's no shame in it."

Payne understood Wade wasn't being kind. He was looking out for himself.

"I'll do my part."

He wasn't sure there was a difference between firing the gun and driving anyway. From the gal back home in the factory making bombs to the sailor who shipped it to Sicily to the tanker who drove the tank to the gunner who fired the shell, nobody's hands were really clean in this war.

"Killing a man is hard as hell, but it gets easier each time," the gunner said. "It gets a whole lot easier when some German tanker has you in his crosshairs and it comes down to you or him. If it helps, make that guy an idea you can hate. You aren't shooting some shoemaker from Hamburg; you're blasting Hitler, fascism. Get mad. That's how you fight from within. Anything else, don't think about too hard."

Payne absorbed all this and said nothing.

"All right." Wade returned to his letter. "Maybe you can help me out, seeing as you're a bit of a philosopher. I have to answer a question yes or no. I don't really want to say yes, but if I do, it'll give me something to fight for."

"It'll give you hope?"

"Yes. An idea to live for, not kill for."

Payne thought about it. "Hope is always good. But I'll give you your own advice right back to you. Write back whatever answer helps you survive."

"I wish I knew what that was," the gunner said.

Payne spotted a line of vehicles approaching the airfield from the south. "Are we expecting company? There's a lot of tanks on the way."

"That's the rest of the regiment."

Payne drove onto the airfield and parked by his platoon. "Home, Sergeant."

"Mm," Wade said, engrossed in his letter.

He'd come back just in time. The entire company was gathering around Captain Ratliff.

"The captain called everybody together," Payne said.

The gunner didn't look up. "Uh-huh."

Payne let the tank idle before turning off the ignition switch. He opened the battery switch, closed the main fuel supply valves, applied the parking brake, and pulled himself out.

The tankers were groaning.

"That's right," Ratliff said. "We did such a good job taking the airfield, the colonel wants Destroyer Company in the lead."

Payne found Russo and nudged him. "What's going on?"

"We're going west to Canicatti while the Big Red One pushes north."

"Why is that bad?"

"Because we just fought and need a rest, numbnuts."

"I thought we were going to Enna," Payne said. "Cut the Italian army in two and put us in line to Messina."

"Yeah, well, we have to take Canicatti first."

"If you're tired, pop a Benzedrine," Ratliff shouted at his company. "Any other complaints, save it for the chaplain. If you want to kill some Heinies, don't do a damn thing, because you're in the right place. Mount up!"

This call to arms over, the crowd broke up to return to their M4s. The tankers trudged the whole way grumbling, but they had a little swagger in their step, flush with combat baptism and victory. They were bitching, but they appeared happy to be moving again. Where they went didn't matter, since it was all Sicily. They just wanted to get it over with, and they now had confidence they could smash anything in their way.

Payne wiggled into his seat behind the bow gun and plugged his headset into his control box in time to say, "Bog, check."

"Destroyers 2, this is Destroyers 2 Actual," the radio droned. "Start your engines. Stand by to move out and march on First Platoon."

"Damn helmet," Ackley bitched. "Like an oven for your brain."

"What do you think?" Payne asked him.

"About what, *Payne*?" Ackley had a way of saying a name as if it was an insult.

"All this." He gestured around him.

The kid guffawed. "Why would I do that?"

Payne shrugged. "Just making conversation."

"If your conversing has anything to do with keeping me alive, speak up."

He bristled but ended up shrugging again. As a New Yorker, he knew how to take a punch.

"Patton wants a port to land troops and supplies," Russo said over the interphone. "Porto Empedocle, the key to which is Agrigento. The doughs are getting set to take it. We'll be taking Canicatti north of it to protect their flank."

"So it was all-important to take Enna until it wasn't," Swanson said.

"Canicatti will get us there too. This is just a detour."

"I heard the Krauts brought in two more divisions onto the island. We're gonna have Tigers, 88s, paratroopers, and Screaming Meemies waiting for us up ahead."

"I heard the Germans were retreating northeast

toward Messina," Russo said.

Wade said, "Did you guys hear anything about some of our doughs shooting prisoners?"

This triggered a flurry of shouted debate. Payne stayed out of it.

The company unwound onto an ancient, narrow road that snaked through the hills to the northwest. As the air filled with dust, Payne pulled his goggles over his eyes.

In granny gear, Dog mounted the first tall hill, offering a spectacular view of the countryside covered in agave, carob trees, and eucalyptus. The air was fragrant with thyme and wildflowers. Blue butterflies danced among the plants.

"Beautiful." Payne pictured how it'd translate on canvas.

"Every time we have a nice view, everybody for miles around has got a nice view of us," Ackley said. "We're sitting ducks up here."

"Can I do anything about that?"

"Nope."

"Then shut up and let me enjoy it without you crapping on it."

Thankfully, Ackley did. Payne had learned the hard way not to make conversation with him.

With the road shimmering in the heat, Dog went down the steep incline as carefully as it had climbed. If a tank slipped and skidded out of control, it could slam into the tank ahead of it, which would be a disaster.

Pierce's voice popped onto the radio. "Destroyers 2, this is Destroyers 2 Actual. Contacts to the south, friendly planes."

"About time they pulled their weight," Wade said.

Shadows flickered across the tank as the planes snarled overhead. Payne smiled as he watched them go. The P38 Lightning was an odd-looking duck, but the P51 Mustang was a beautiful bird of prey.

"I should have been a pilot," Payne said. He imagined riding the atmosphere in a humming winged machine, howling toward the ground in a dive.

The planes banked and turned to the west.

"It's good to have air cover," Russo said.

"They're coming back," Payne said. "You can hear it in the pitch."

"Toss a yellow smoke."

"A what?"

"Smoke grenade. It's under Wade's seat. It signals we're friendly. Let's not take any chances."

Wade passed it to Payne, who pulled the pin and tossed it onto the side of the road. Yellow smoke hissed in an expanding cloud. Despite the signal, the Mustangs screamed low toward the column.

Then they opened up with their .50-caliber machine guns.

"Driver, stop," Russo shouted. "Everybody, button up!"

Payne dropped his seat and pulled the hatch after him as the rounds ricocheted off the tanks' heavy armor. An explosion boomed somewhere in the column's rear.

"*Che cozz, gidrul?*" Russo cried.

The ground trembled with the concussion of bombs. Dust and stone pinged off Dog's armor. The

Lightning was getting in on the action.

The commander was raving now. "*Giamocc, scustumad—*"

"Shut up, Mac," Swanson said. "I can't hear the bombs."

The air filled with engine howl as the Mustangs dived for another strafing run. Slugs thudded against Dog's armor, ripped through the baggage stowed on the rear deck, and chewed the stones.

The roar of the planes faded to a plaintive snarl.

"Destroyers 2, this is Destroyers 2 Actual," Pierce said, his voice strained with barely concealed rage. "It appears our friendly air forces can't see the white stars on our tanks and just blew up our gasoline truck."

The tankers groaned at this news.

"Planes leaving on southerly course. All tanks, move out on First Platoon."

"I just hope we ain't in range of the Navy's guns," Swanson said.

The men opened the hatches only to stiffen at the growl of an aircraft engine.

"Contact, German plane," Pierce said. "Looks like a Messerschmitt. All tanks stop! Unlimber the fifties and shoot it down!"

"Oh, I will," Russo fumed as he hauled himself out of the cupola. Moments later, he was screaming his head off as he blazed away at the sky. The shooting thrummed through the turret. Empty shell casings pinged off the hull.

"Are we there yet?" Swanson shouted.

After three strafing runs, the commander dropped

back into the turret and ordered Dog forward.

Until American planes showed up again to take another crack at the column.

CHAPTER ELEVEN

CANICATTI

Tank Sergeant Wade wanted to shoot something.

The column had road-marched twenty-five miles over the hills while enduring alternating waves of American and German plane strafe and bomb runs. The attacks produced few casualties but a whole lot of fury, as it seemed both militaries were now in cahoots against them. After fighting for forty-eight hours on little sleep, the tankers were running on fumes and Benzedrine.

Second and Third Platoons stood behind a ridge overlooking a rolling valley that led to Canicatti, a town of thirty thousand people. Shouldered by tall hills, it bottlenecked the road north to Enna and south to Agrigento. Just four miles away, but during a twilight probe last night, First Platoon had lost three tanks to Italian Semovente 90s in a village along the route.

The Semovente 90 self-propelled anti-aircraft gun was a typical Italian tank, shoddy and lightly armored, but its gun packed a hell of a punch. Behind Destroyer Company, artillery was setting up a barrage. Ratliff wanted in on it. The captain was out there on the ridge hunched behind a tripod-mounted MG sight, working its azimuth and elevation knobs.

Wade prepared for indirect fire by laying his

gunner's quadrant on the breech ring and moving its arm until the bubble centered. He then elevated the gun based on range to the crest plus four mils so the bottom of the gun bore cleared the crest.

"Destroyers 2, this is Destroyers 2 Actual," the platoon commander said over the radio. "Stand by for indirect area fire, parallel sheaf."

A parallel sheaf meant shooting in parallel lines, resulting in a uniform bombardment. A burst was thirty yards wide. Three platoons would smash the village with a line of bursts across some four hundred yards, which would destroy the Semoventes or flush them out.

"Civilians live in that village," Payne said.

"Italian tanks are in that village," Wade pointed out. "And the Italian army put them there. That's on them, not us."

"I can't believe I'm saying this, but the Professor is right," Swanson said.

Russo's response was strained. "It's on General Guzzoni. Yeah."

"Kill or be killed, right," the bog said. "Congrats, you can go home and live a long and happy life carrying all that killing with you. It'll be a great life."

"Tell us something we don't know," Ackley said.

"We either shoot, or we go home," Wade said.

The loader considered that idea. "Well, when I hear it put that way, maybe New Guy's onto something. I still don't know why we're fighting a European war."

"Because you volunteered for it, *boombots*," Russo said. "We either beat the Nazis here or we'll be fighting them in New—"

With resounding booms, the two platoon leaders' tanks fired a salvo of one spotting round each, two seconds apart.

"Well, that decides that," Wade said.

They would be shooting, and soon. He couldn't wait. He'd written his letter to Alice saying he wanted to save their marriage. The decision had given him not so much happiness as catharsis. A profound sense of relief. He didn't have to wrestle with his marriage's uncertainty anymore. He could just give in and ride the choice wherever it took him.

He hadn't V-mailed the letter yet, but with the decision made, he wanted to go home and see how things worked out. This longing was like a physical need, the kind of thing men get stupid and go AWOL for. If he wouldn't have to swim across the Atlantic, he would have already started walking home.

That left one option, which was to fight hard until the Germans threw in the towel. Wade understood disaster might be waiting for him back in Minneapolis. He and Alice would make up, and things would be great a while. Maybe they'd try to have a baby with the thought it'd tie them together. But the mistrust would always be there, eating at him. Still, he had to go see for himself. He had to get to her before she changed her mind. A physical need.

Ratliff called in adjustments. Wade worked his hand wheels to fine tune elevation and direction.

"Welcome to the artillery," Pierce said. "Platoon, ten rounds, fire for effect. Make it rain."

"On the way," Wade said and stepped on the firing pedal.

The tank shook from the blast and recoil. The round whistled as it arced over the crest and onto the village. The shell casing clanged out as the breech jumped back. Wade caught a strong whiff of gunpowder. The fan sucked the resulting smoke out of the turret.

Swanson loaded another HE round. "Up, Prof."

"On the way."

"New Guy don't want to get his hands dirty." The loader shoved in another round. "You're up."

Dog bucked as the next HE round shot out of the gun.

Wade didn't have a problem with Payne. Out of everybody in his crew—including John Austin and Eugene Clay—Payne was the only man who'd joined up for a reason that wasn't selfish. Austin had his family honor, Clay had something to prove to himself, Russo wanted to make a showing as a good American, and he and Swanson had escaped bad situations back home. Payne wasn't even doing it out of patriotism. It wasn't love of country but love for his fellow man that made him fight. He wanted humanity to live without fascism.

He just hadn't prepared himself to kill for it.

"He'll find his way," Wade said. "Don't act like you showed up in Algeria happy to kill human beings."

"But I still did it," the loader countered. "We all did."

"And so will he. If you don't like it, don't take it out on him."

"I ain't—"

"Anyway, he drove the tank during the attack on the

airfield, while you loaded. What's the difference? The only born killer we had on the crew was Clay, and he's gone. So quit acting like you're some big warrior now."

For once, Swanson kept his big yap shut.

Russo said, "Check fire. That was ten rounds."

"Outstanding fire mission, Destroyers 2," Pierce said over the radio. "The captain says we hit them hard. Start engines, and stand by to move out."

Ackley ignited the engine, which responded with a growl. Boots thudded on the hull as armored infantry clambered aboard for the assault.

"Pass me rounds from stowage for the ready rack, New Guy," Swanson said.

"Driver, move out on Delilah," Russo ordered.

Destroyer Company rolled over the ridge into the valley. Smoke plumed lazily from the shattered village. From here, through his scope, Wade could see all the way to Canicatti and its thirty thousand souls.

"Come on," he muttered to himself. "Let's do this."

Bolstering Wade's eagerness for battle was the understanding that every yard he drove farther from home brought him closer to it.

With sweeping turrets and primed guns, the tanks columned through the devastated village. Wade took in harvested wheat filling a barn with a stove-in roof, houses partially reduced to rubble. Pale faces peered out in terror from the ruins. Women, children, old men.

"Where are they?" Russo growled.

The commander wasn't just looking for something to shoot. Wade understood he wanted the barrage to have had a useful purpose.

Standing behind a berm in a cratered vineyard, a burned-out Semovente came into view. Wade and Russo let out a sigh together.

"We got one," the commander said.

The column cleared the village and formed a line a mile abreast on the valley floor before continuing toward Canicatti. Their little bells ringing, a flock of sheep bleated and scurried out of the way of the snorting metal beasts. Expecting the Germans to open up any minute, the company bounded forward by platoon, each platoon always covering the others with loaded 75s.

Russo dropped into the turret and pulled his hatch closed. "Incoming!"

Shells whistled out of the ether. The concussions trembled through the hull. The armored infantry scrambled off the tank to find cover.

"We just lost our doughs," Wade said.

"Stupid," Swanson said. "Now they're gonna have to walk through the rain to get there. They was better off with us."

"Orders, I think," Wade said. "Dismount at first sign of trouble."

"Dumb orders, you ask me."

"Keep it moving," Pierce said over the radio.

"Balls to the wall, Ackley," Russo said. "Evasive maneuver!"

Engine whining in high gear, Dog zigzagged the last mile toward the town. With each passing moment, the tile-roofed stone buildings in Wade's scope grew larger. A shell burst fifty yards ahead and hurled a wave of dirt that obscured his view. Dog zigged to the right and maintained speed, barely missing a collision with Dealer. Angry chatter filled the radio.

"What are we doing?" Wade said in rising panic. "We have no support."

Tanks were the rooks of the chessboard, mobile forts mounted with cannons, ideally suited to battering the enemy and supporting infantry across open spaces. However, they were highly vulnerable to infantry antitank weapons in cramped urban streets, and Wade figured the town ahead would be crammed with them.

"I don't know," Russo said.

"Destroyers 2, form a column behind Delilah," Pierce ordered. "We're going to drive through as fast as we can. Get on your fifties and keep a sharp eye. Word is the town's filled with snipers and AT guns."

"*Fanabola*," Russo snarled as he climbed out to unlimber the machine gun.

"You're up, Payne," Wade said. "You see somebody, you shoot."

"All I see are white sheets hanging from windows," the bog said.

"The town is surrendering. The Germans, however, don't care what the townspeople want. You see anybody wearing a uniform, you shoot him dead."

In three columns, the tank platoons hurtled at top speed into Canicatti and immediately opened up with everything they had.

"Who's shooting?" Wade said.

"Everybody," Russo yelled back. "They're lighting

up the town."

The turret filled with the crash of guns. The lead tanks sent shells into second-story windows while the .50-cals raked them. Flaming furniture and chunks of masonry belched into the street and were crushed by the tracks.

Delilah fired a delayed-fuse HE round into the intersection ahead, which exploded into a screen of dust that concealed their passage.

"Gunner, traverse left," Russo shouted over the roar. "Building coming up on our nine. Put an HE round through the front door."

"Fuck you, Tony," Wade said. "I'm not doing your massacre!"

"It's got a flag and graffiti on it." That marked it as a government building, possibly the local fascist headquarters.

"Goddamn it." He traversed the turret and reduced elevation to lay the gun at door level. "The gun is set."

"You're up, Professor," Swanson said.

Wade still hesitated. "We shoot this close, we could damage Dog."

Russo dropped back into the turret and buttoned up. "It's a legit target, and we're taking it out. Fire when ready."

"Fine!" Wade waited until the door was just about in his reticle. "On the way!"

The gun spat a shell with a burst of flame. The door and surrounding wall disappeared in a flash, vomiting rubble and a wave of dust across the street ahead. Baseball-sized chunks of masonry rattled like hail off

Dog's armor.

"Scratch one fascist HQ," the commander said. "Dog's fine."

The explosions outside amplified as the column emerged on the other side of Canicatti and mounted the high ground to the north.

"Give it a rest, boys," Swanson said.

"That's the Germans," Wade said. "They're dropping arty on the town."

"Well, that's even peachier for the folks here."

"Shut up about the civilians, Animal," Russo snarled. "And that goes double for you, Payne. We don't need anybody to be our conscience. We already got one. This isn't surgery; civilians are gonna get killed. We can't do anything about it, so we don't need to think about it while we're doing our jobs. If you get upset, tell it to GI Jesus. All of you, get your thick heads in the game."

"Roger," Payne said.

Wade turned and nodded his approval. "Roger that, Tony."

"You don't need to tell me," Ackley said. "You're a bunch of babies."

"Of course we don't need to tell you, Ack-Ack," Swanson said, "because you're a goddamn psycho."

The kid laughed. "You guys are like Rommel when it comes to beating yourselves—"

"SHUT UP," Russo screamed. "We're in combat. Heads in the game. Now."

"Destroyers 2, this is Destroyers 2 Actual," the radio blared. "I'm taking AT fire from the crest. Spread out and engage until the doughs catch up."

Wade spotted a muzzle flash and puff of smoke from a sandbagged position in the rocks near the top of the hill, about twenty-five hundred yards away. "I got him on our two."

"Driver, clock one and march for that stone wall," Russo ordered.

"All right."

"We need cover. They're thick as fleas up there."

Dog rumbled up the rocky slope past a lemon orchard and stopped beside Delilah, which was already banging away at the antitank guns on the heights.

"Up," Swanson said. "We're down to about twenty rounds of the HE."

Russo flinched in the cupola as a ricochet clanged against Dog's hull. "They're throwing everything they've got against Delilah."

"Who's up there, Mac? The ginzos?"

"No. Krauts. I think we just found the 15th Panzergrenadiers. Time to make Dog bark. Gunner, antitank, HE, two-five hundred!"

"Ready!"

"Fire!"

Wade slammed his foot down. "On the way!"

Dog barked and shot a round toward the target. The shell burst far short.

"Up ten, right ten, fire!"

Wade worked the hand wheels. "On the way!"

Dog boomed. A second later, shrapnel splashed across its hull. Wade chafed behind the gun. They were in trouble here with a disadvantage in elevation and no infantry support. They were taking plunging fire and needed to get on high ground.

"Delilah's hit!" Russo said. "She took a hit on the gun barrel. It spun the turret around. The shell bounced off the front plate and turned it glowing hot. Wait—the gunner's out."

Wade turned to glare at Russo. "Correct my fire, or I'll do it myself."

"Target's obscured by smoke—*Payne!* What are you doing?"

A shiver ran down Wade's spine despite the maddening heat. Things were going to hell quickly. "What's going on?"

"He just bailed!"

"What?"

"Run, you coward!" Ackley called after him.

"He's going to Delilah," Russo said. "He's helping get the crew out. The lieutenant's got a busted wing... Now he's getting the loader out. The man's got a Tommy gun for a splint—*managgia*! Delilah took another hit and is burning!"

The radio exploded in panicked voices. Artillery shells slammed around the tanks with explosions that shook the ground.

"That's our own artillery shooting at us!" Butter howled on the radio.

Knuckles rapped on Dog's hull. "Help me up, goddamn it!"

Wade started in his chair. It was the lieutenant.

"I'm going back for the loader," Payne shouted outside.

"This is Destroyers 2 Actual," Pierce said, his

voice taut with pain from his broken arm. "Clear the frequency! This is Destroyers 2 Actual. Everybody, fire Willy Pete at the hilltop and pull back to the edge of town. We'll use the buildings as cover until the doughs catch up."

"Roger," the other tank commanders called out.

"About time," Swanson growled. Wade had to agree.

"Gunner," Russo called out. "Willy Pete, antitank, traverse right, range two-five hundred, steady, on! Fire!"

Wade stomped the pedal. "On the way!"

The white phosphorous shell burst and sprayed a thick cloud of brilliant white smoke. Shrapnel cracked against Dog's hull as another artillery shell exploded nearby. A shot from a German gun blurred past Wade's scope.

"Gunner, Willy Pete, antitank, traverse left, two-eight hundred, steady, steady, on! Fire!"

"On the way!"

The rest of the platoon had gotten in on the action. Enemy fire slackened as dense clouds of smoke hovered along the crest.

"Delilah's whole crew is loaded on our deck," Russo said. "Payne found a ladder from the orchard to use as a stretcher for the loader. Driver, reverse."

"Damn it," Wade said, though things hadn't turned out too badly, all things considered. Still, he fumed at the idea of retreat. The mad charge across the valley had been cathartic. The pell-mell rush through the town. No matter what both armies threw at them, planes and artillery strikes, they'd pushed through and kept rolling. He'd wanted to keep advancing until he'd made it all the way home, but the war was no longer obliging.

The Germans had just stopped them cold. And having stonewalled the Americans, Wade knew it was only a matter of time before they counterattacked.

CHAPTER TWELVE

SIDELINED

Corporal Swanson nipped from his bottle of gin and belched.

"*Maronna mia*," Russo said in the turret's dim, muggy interior. "At least try to hide it."

Swanson was bone-tired and didn't care right now if the Nazis were marching through Washington, DC. At the same time, he'd gladly strangle a Nazi with his bare hands if it won him some shuteye.

He took another nip.

"All right, give me a snort," Russo said. The loader handed the gin over.

After D Company had fallen back, E Company moved west onto the high ground and flanked the antitank guns, which freed the Destroyers to resume their advance. F Company sidled into position on D's right. Infantry advanced.

Then, with Pierce and his Delilah out of commission, Ratliff made the blunder of temporarily appointing Russo platoon commander. Ol' Mac had himself the bright idea of pushing out along the main access road at night and bunkering down for an ambush.

"You know they ain't coming," Swanson said. "We could be sleeping right now."

"How could you sleep after the day we've had?"

"I'm dying to sleep because you won't let me. If you tell me I'm allowed to sleep, I won't be able to."

The commander chuckled. "I think I can relate."

"Four roads into town, and we're on the wrong one. I can feel it."

"But only one road from the north, numbnuts. Where the Germans are."

"Giant waste of time," Swanson said, refusing to let Mac have the last word.

He pushed his hatch open and squeezed his torso through for a breath of cool, fresh air. Dog sat in an olive grove with its 75 pointed at the road. A company of doughs rested around the tank, waiting for something to happen. Somewhere out there, an armored infantry recon squad knelt behind a stone wall with orders to signal the tanks when the enemy approached.

Crickets and katydids sang in the dark. Ripe olives fell from the trees, splattering and plunking against Dog's armor. In the distance, a pair of canines barked. The air smelled like the usual Sicilian cocktail of honeysuckle, jasmine, and sheep shit. A plane hummed somewhere in a night sky full of stars.

"Destroyers 2 Actual, this is Destroyers 2-2," Cranston said over the radio. "The infantry are signaling me there are vehicles approaching."

"Let me know when you have eyes on them," Russo said. "Follow the plan."

"Roger."

"Destroyers 2 Actual, out."

Swanson sensed the commander gloating.

"Looks like the Krauts are coming after all," Russo

said.

"Ducky," Swanson said.

"What do you want me to do when we start shooting?" Payne said.

"Try shooting the Krauts, New Guy."

"But we have our own guys somewhere ahead of us."

Russo climbed out of the turret and unlimbered the .50. "The recon element is bugging out. You'll have clear firing lanes."

"You should also stay in the tank, New Guy," Swanson added. "You'll live longer."

"What were you thinking, jumping out like that?" Ackley said.

"I'm the bog," Payne said. "It's my job to leave the tank when needed. The lieutenant was hit. You'd have done the same in my shoes."

Swanson laughed. "Are you serious?"

"If we were hit, you'd want somebody to help get you out, right?"

The laughter faded. "I guess I would. You're an odd duck, New Guy. But you walk the talk, I'll give you that much."

"Ask me before you do it next time," Russo said. "Dog comes first."

"Roger."

"Now everybody shut it. Vehicles are approaching."

Swanson tensed behind Wade, who sat hunched at the 75. The plan was simple enough even this platoon of knuckleheads could get it right. Dog knocking out the first vehicle was the signal for Cranston to knock out the last, and then the platoon would light up everything trapped in between.

Cranston relayed everything he saw over the radio. Armored cars, light trucks, antitank guns, gasoline trucks. No tanks.

"They're coming on now," Russo replied. "Everybody, stand by to fire."

Swanson peered into his scope. Through the trees, black shapes growled along the road. Usually, he hated when Russo was right. The little runt's head was big enough already, and Swanson took a perverse pleasure in seeing him bashed down to size, even if it meant him suffering too.

He didn't mind it this time, though. In fact, he couldn't believe this was actually happening. They really had the drop on the Germans. If Russo's plan worked, it'd be an old-fashioned turkey shoot.

"Make your shots count, Professor," he said. "We're running low on ammo."

"I hear you."

Russo stiffened behind his .50. "Gunner, armored car, HE, two-five-zero, lead one-zero, stand by." His voice was quiet and terse.

Swanson already had a round in the breech. "Up."

"I've got him," Wade said.

"Fire when you've got a sure shot."

"On the way."

Dog roared with a flash that lit up the trees and the German column. The shell punched the armored car above the rear wheels and spun the disintegrating, flaming wreck. Another three booms echoed Dog's shot as the rest of the platoon loosed a volley. Russo opened up with the .50.

"Hit! Gunner, truck, HE, follow my burst! Fire!"

Swanson wrenched his eyes from his scope and shoved another HE round into the breech. "Up!"

"On the way!"

Dog boomed again.

"Hit!" Russo crowed. "*Maronna mia*, it's like shooting fish in a barrel! Work your way down the line, Wade!" He howled into the hot wind of a fireballing gasoline truck. "Let 'em have it!"

Dog laid down devastating fire with every gun it had while Swanson rammed round after round into the smoking breech. HE, Willy Pete, AP, everything they had left. The flashes of bursts and tracers strobed through the viewports. Machine gun rounds hammered the front plate.

"Bog, doughs, right front, fire!"

Without hesitation, the new guy burned through a belt and yelled, "Reloading!"

The enemy machine gun fire stopped.

"Destroyers 2, this is Destroyers 2 Actual," Russo shouted into the radio. "Move out toward the road. Get the doughs moving. Let's bag some prisoners. He switched to INT and added, "Driver, move out."

"All right," Ackley said.

"Friendlies all around now, bog. Fire only if you're sure."

"Roger."

Swanson grinned into his scope as the tank stopped near the road. The armored infantry was rounding up prisoners, scores of figures silhouetted by burning vehicles. He counted around ten enemy vehicles destroyed, another fifteen intact but abandoned.

"Gentlemen," Russo announced. "We just kicked the 15th Panzergrenadiers' ass."

"*Duce*," the loader replied, "you might just be getting the knack for this."

"I'm leaving the tank," Payne said and went outside to throw up.

Swanson expected a hero's welcome when the platoon and its armored infantry returned to Canicatti with more than two hundred Germans and fifteen vehicles in the bag, and this time he wasn't disappointed. Even Ratliff was impressed.

Hands on his hips, the captain beamed with something resembling pride. "You guys did good."

Filthy and exhausted, every member of the platoon smiled as they mingled among their scarred and battered tanks. If they hadn't felt like an elite fighting force before with their painted turrets and earlier win at Dirillo Bridge, they sure did now.

"Those guns you hear up on the bluffs is one of our sister companies taking the pass," Ratliff went on. "Once it's in our hands, the army will have a clear road anywhere it wants to go in Sicily. But not us."

The smiles turned into hopeful grins.

"They're taking us off the line," Swanson murmured, more a prayer than a guess.

"The 15th Infantry is coming into our area of operations," the captain told them. "Once they're set up, we'll be going back the way we came to an assembly area near Campobello." A town of ten thousand souls about five miles southeast of Canicatti. "We'll be on reserve for the near future."

The tankers cheered and returned to their tanks for chow.

Swanson found the Coleman and set it on the ground. He locked the stove's arms in place, attached a metal ring to them, and set a pot on the ring. "I'm sick of the meat hash. I'll have the meat and vegetable stew tonight."

"The paper labels all fell off," Payne called back as he rustled around for C rations. "You get what you get."

"Ducky. Just grab five cans, and bring them out here."

Wade plopped down and set up a second stove. "I'm sick of all of them."

"No fancy dinners for you no more, Professor."

"I don't expect fine cuisine in the Army," Wade fumed, his face reddening. "But I can expect not to eat the same goddamn thing every goddamn day while I'm getting shot at for Uncle Sam."

"I'll bring it up with Patton next time I see him." Swanson opened his can and sighed. Meat and potato hash. "Anybody want to trade?"

He had no takers, so he spooned the gunk into his pot. Payne added his meat and beans to Wade's so he could use his own stove to boil water for coffee. They all tried not to look at Ackley, who always ate his C rations cold and managed to smear some around his mouth.

Swanson shook his head at the sight of him. "And

they call me Animal."

Russo walked over and sat with the crew. "I just talked to the captain. He wanted me to pass on what a great job he thinks we did with that ambush."

The loader pumped the stove's lever to pressurize the fuel and lit it. "Yeah, we just heard him say that, Mac."

"I'll be staying on as platoon commander for a while."

"Ducky. That means Dog's on point, and everybody will be shooting at us."

"How's the lieutenant?" Payne asked.

"His arm got busted up pretty good," Russo said. "The loader's leg broke when the turret jerked to the left. They're okay but out of the war for a while."

"Good for them."

"You did good last night, Payne. You were pretty cool on the bow gun."

Swanson sampled his lukewarm meat hash and let it continue to cook. "New Guy popped his cherry."

Payne paled and gazed at his meal with sudden loathing. "I guess I did."

"I was thinking up some plans," Russo said. "We need a better way to talk to the infantry outside the tank. And we need a way to make sure friendly planes don't hit us again. Maybe flags on the aerials or something."

Swanson was already sorry he'd complimented the man last night. "Lord, you're turning into an eager beaver, ain't you?"

"I'm just trying to—"

"Those are good ideas, Tony," Wade said. "Tell the

captain."

"This is—"

"Really swell ideas," Swanson cut in. "Tell the captain."

Russo took the hint and opened his can. "Meat and beans again!"

"Want to trade? I've got meat hash here."

Russo eyed Swanson's bubbling pot bleakly. Neither appealed to him. "All right. You already heated it up, so I guess I'll take it."

Ackley smacked his lips over his can. "Meat and beans. Yum, yum."

"Save it, Ackley," Wade said. "It's hard enough eating this dog food without seeing you get it all over your face."

"No more wakey-wakey pills for you, Ack-Ack," Swanson chimed in. "Them pep pills are ruining what little you had for a brain."

After chow, the bleary-eyed tankers topped up on fuel and heavy oil, tightened the tracks, and lubed the 75. Before the bedrolls could be unhitched, Ratliff ordered the company to move out. Ackley was coming down off his Benzedrine and could barely walk, much less drive. While the kid snored loudly in the bog seat, Payne took the sticks for the five-mile road march to the assembly area northwest of Campobello di Licata.

"They set up tents for us," Russo said at the cupola, the heady responsibilities of platoon command keeping him annoyingly wide awake. "We might be staying here a while."

"Fine by me," Swanson said. "I'm gonna sleep a

week."

Dog parked where told. While the tank was still idling, Swanson hauled himself through his hatch and untied his bedroll.

"Driver, cut the engine." Russo swelled in the cupola as he surveyed the bivouac. "First thing's first, men. We need to—"

Swanson stretched out his bedroll. "Yup. I'm gonna sleep now."

He didn't sleep a week, but he gave it his best effort.

From the high ground, Swanson took in Sicily spread before him like a massive, wrinkled blanket. The picturesque little town of Campobello di Licata lay nestled in one of its folds. The world appeared desolate from up here, the town lonely and lost. More than anywhere he'd been in this war, it reminded Swanson of home. He'd always preferred air and space to his fellow man.

"Coming or staying, Animal," Russo called.

"Get your rear in gear," Ackley yelled.

Especially these fellow men.

"Hold your goddamn horses," Swanson growled and moseyed over to the idling deuce-and-a-half, taking his sweet time out of sheer spite. He climbed onto the back of the olive-green truck, and it sped off and mounted the road leading into town.

For two days, the regiment had rested while offering a reserve force able to respond to any major Axis counterattacks on a thirty-minute alert. Aside from the occasional false alarm in the night's witching hours and dogfight in the sky, nothing much happened, and only Reconnaissance Company saw action as it probed the enemy line north of Canicatti.

Swanson was fine with that, enjoying the rest and not being shot at by high-velocity shells. He didn't care much about the big picture because he usually turned out dead wrong when he made any attempt to understand it. The big picture always took care of itself, and it was enough to worry about his own ass parked in a single tank. Then this morning the big picture turned out to be the entire army getting sidelined.

The British commander Montgomery had shunted the Americans off Highway 124 and taken both roads to Messina for himself. For the duration, Seventh Army would twiddle its thumbs while it protected the British Eighth Army's flank. In Swanson's neck of the woods, a man showed appreciation when you saved his empire, but old Monty was full of himself.

Swanson was fine with that too. Sitting the bench offered serious health benefits. The other guys bitched about playing second fiddle to the Brits, who still didn't trust the American fighting man after Kasserine Pass, but national honor didn't add up to a hill of beans for the likes of Swanson, who loved living more than he loved his country. He'd kill for America if he had to, but he wasn't dying for it if he could help it.

Instead, he was going on a mission for the camp mess. A certain high-ranking officer wanted wine and local delicacies for his table, and since Russo spoke the local lingo, he was given a truck from the motor pool and tasked with running the errand into Campobello di Licata. Swanson and the rest of Dog's crew agreed to provide security for the chance to score souvenirs.

"Think about it, *goombahs*," Russo enthused behind the wheel. "Thousands of women are in that town, and their men have been away for years. They're all yours except for one special lady, my future wife."

Swanson loaded a barbed reply concerning the commander's alleged romantic skills, only to stop with widening eyes. What Russo had described sounded like heaven.

This crazy trip to Sicily might have a sunny side after all, he thought.

CHAPTER THIRTEEN

LOVE IS IN THE AIR

Corporal Russo parked the truck in Campobello di Licata's deserted main square and cut the engine. He dismounted and slung his Tommy gun over his shoulder. A church bell tolled, warning the *paesans* to clear the streets because of the invading Americans.

Wade hopped down from the bed. "We're taking a big risk here."

The company remained on a thirty-minute alert. If the Germans counterattacked, or even if there was another false alarm, they'd all be in hot water if they didn't make it back in time.

That and regardless of the white sheets that hung from the windows, the town might still have been hostile. Campobello had already been cleared, but they could never be sure of a territory's safety until a permanent occupation force showed up. Right now, partisan fascist fanatics who wanted to commit suicide by soldier for the fatherland were a bigger worry than enemy soldiers.

"Then let's get to it," Russo said, though he didn't move. His gaze swept the square at the center of what might have been the quaintest town he'd ever seen. Aside from fascist slogans graffitied on some of the walls—*Many Enemies More Honor, Blood Moves the*

Wheels of History, Liberty is Duty—the war hadn't touched this place. Ancient and imposing, a brown sandstone Baroque cathedral dominated the view.

This was his first real visit to the Old Country. *Old* was right; this place felt ancient, its culture and traditions running deep. These buildings had stood here for centuries. He breathed deeply and caught the scents of wild thyme and gladioli.

"See you at 1200," Wade said. "Come on, Leonard."

The tankers walked off to hunt for souvenirs.

"Animal, you're with me," the tank commander said. "Ackley, you stay with the truck."

"All right. As long as I get my share."

Swanson shouldered a box filled with cigarette cartons. They walked across the deserted square and explored the narrow radial streets. Above, clothes drying on lines were strung between buildings.

"Thousands of women, huh?" the loader said. "I don't see anybody."

Russo shook his head. "If an army of Italian women invaded your country, would you rush out and have sex with them?"

Swanson stared at him. "Wouldn't you?"

"Women are not men. They are soft and gentle. They have to be wooed."

"You don't know a damn thing about women." Seeing Russo bluster, the loader added, "Relax, Mac. I don't get them neither."

"I'm Sicilian. Love is like breathing to us." Before Swanson could reply, Russo pointed. "There's the shop. Come on."

The loader snorted. "Whatever you say, Mac."

Private First Class Payne sauntered along a street and paused to admire a wall embellished with terracotta. "What a beautiful place."

Wade scanned their surroundings. "I was hoping for an open-air market. If the locals are too scared to come out, I guess we're limited to sightseeing."

Payne snapped a picture with his Brownie. "Fine with me."

"In that case, I know where I want to go. I'll see you back at the truck." The gunner walked off.

"Aren't we supposed to stick together?"

"You'll be okay. Just keep your finger near the trigger on that Tommy."

Payne watched Wade walk away. He'd spent weeks with him and three other men who, on a daily basis, tested his patience four ways from Sunday. He'd had to breathe their farts, suffer through their snoring, and listen to them chew.

Finally free of them and the suffocating tracked oven they called Dog, he felt alone and exposed. When he was with the crew, he was annoyed much of the time, but he was safe.

Then he took a deep breath and sighed it out, getting over it. Yes, alone at last. Happiness washed over him along with something more profound: relief.

Being alone was just fine.

He wandered the cobblestone streets, drinking it all in until he found himself mounting a rise. In the shade of a lemon tree garden, he had a clear view across the slanted red-tiled roofs of the sandstone buildings to a barren hill on the other side of town, where a lonely cluster of Doric columns supported a shard of pediment. A solitary figure was climbing to visit this ancient temple.

Of course that's where Wade would want to go. Payne admired the way the gunner retained his passion even during the war. The way he scavenged and traded books to devour during the long tedium. War had a way of eating a man's humanity, but it hadn't gotten Wade's yet.

Payne explored the garden and discovered a standing easel with a stretched canvas mounted on it. Paints, a bowl of fruit, and a pitcher of wine rested on a small table. Somebody had been painting before the Americans showed up and the church bells rang. He walked over expecting to see a work in progress, but the canvas was blank, as if presented just for him as some kind of tailored peace offering.

Wade had the right idea. Going to war did not have to mean putting your passions on hold; one could even use the war to explore them. Payne had discovered a horrible beauty in combat, building inspiration but offering no real release. Since painting the aggressive cartoons on the tank turrets, he hadn't created anything. Lucky for him, he'd invaded a country with a deep appreciation for art.

Nobody around. He'd make his trade and hope his own offering was acceptable. Cigarettes for one canvas, a little paint, a sip of this wine.

The painter had his oils laid out with an impressive array of brushes. Payne didn't have much time and would have to adapt his technique accordingly.

Normally, he'd paint layer on layer while allowing the paint to dry between layers, and he'd build his vision with as many as sixty layers. Instead, he'd have to use an *alla prima* technique, a direct, wet-on-wet style favored by the impressionist masters like Monet and van Gogh.

He set down his submachine gun and a carton of Camels and picked up a brush that would make a broad stroke. Payne became so engrossed he didn't notice he was no longer alone.

Another brush, held by a female hand, extended toward the canvas.

Russo tried the door, but it was locked.

"Maybe they're all sleeping," Swanson said.

"Siesta isn't for another couple of hours." Russo banged on the thick wood.

The door cracked open, and a pale face peered out. "*Se?*"

"*Bon jornu*," Russo beamed. "*Mi chiamu* Anthony Russo."

"*Signore* Scicolone," the gaunt man introduced himself in a guarded tone, no doubt wondering what this was about. "*Piaciri di canuscìriti.*"

The introductions and common courtesies over, Russo explained he had cigarettes and wanted to trade. The man opened the door and welcomed them inside with a satisfied smile.

"Plenty to buy here," the man said in Sicilian, which spiced its Latin with Greek, Arabic, French, Catalan, and Spanish. He gestured to the woman standing beside a sack of dry goods. "Permit me to introduce my daughter, Ignazia."

The girl wore a traditional black skirt and white blouse with a shawl wrapped around her shoulders. Her hair was done up in a neat bun. She had an oval face, full lips, and large, glittering black eyes.

Russo bowed, his heart pounding. "Pleased to meet you, *Signora.*"

Signore Scicolone offered a tour of the goods he had available while sizing up the boxes of cigarettes the Americans had brought him. As with the rest of Sicily, food was rationed and luxuries like chocolate had become almost non-existent, but there were staples an American soldier put a high value on, such as wine, herbs, and onions. Meanwhile, the U.S. Army had plenty of good cigarettes, which for a heavily rationed country like Italy had become so valuable that they could be used as a common currency. The makings of a fair trade.

While they haggled over the deal, Swanson leered at Ignazia, who glared back at him coldly before ignoring him altogether. In his awkward, boyish manner, the loader made his way closer until he had her cornered.

"Um," he said. "I'm Amos."

The maid whipped her head back and made a *ntze* sound. It looked like acknowledgment, though Russo knew better, recognizing the dismissive gesture from growing up in a Sicilian family.

"*Sono attratto,*" Swanson declared, reciting the new phrase Russo had taught him with the elegance of a child failing at a spelling bee. "*C'abballi cu mia?*"

The woman stared at him in astonishment. Swanson

had just told her he was attracted to her and had asked her to dance.

The loader's face turned scarlet in the ensuing silence, which stretched to the point of hostility. "What did I say, Mac?"

"This one's taken, Animal," Russo said.

Sweating now, Swanson said, "*M'av'a scusari.*"

With this apology, the loader stomped through the door to wait outside. Counting cigarette packs, Signore Scicolone hadn't noticed the exchange. Russo smiled at Ignazia. She turned away with haughty indifference, though she flashed him a coy glance. His heart pounded as they played this game throughout the transaction, him admiring her, her ignoring him like a cat until she eyed him as one did a mouse.

Fortune had smiled on him. *This was the girl.* She wandered the periphery of the room, hips swishing to offer a glimpse of scarlet petticoat under her skirt.

Signore Scicolone opened a bottle of wine and poured out two tall glasses. "The deal is fair. We will drink to our business."

The deal wasn't exactly fair. Sicily was so poor a pack of cigarettes would probably buy him the whole town and everything in it. But Russo wanted to grease the skids with Ignazia's father.

He raised his glass. "Â *saluti, Signore.*"

"Â *saluti!*"

He gazed at the woman again while he drank.

Ignazia. Her name meant *fire.* This aristocratic woman would spice his life and give him companionship and sometimes make his life hell, and in return he'd honor and serve her and love every minute of it.

Yes, she was the one. He just knew.

From the sly smirk she let slip past her lips, Russo could tell she knew it too.

The woman offered Payne a devious grin. "*Ciau, Americano.*"

He smiled back. "Hello."

Her gaze returned to the canvas, which he'd broadstroked with thinned paint to block out the general shapes and colors. Red roofs, brown hill, blue sky. She wore a simple sundress that revealed tanned arms flecked with paint, giving him the impression this was no idle hobby for her.

"Hmm," she said, trying to catch his vision in this raw beginning.

Payne continued blocking. The woman added to his layering with her own bold *impasto* strokes, laying on the paint thick to produce an added sense of dimension to the foreground elements. His focus on the canvas tensed against his animal awareness of her proximity. When their arms accidentally brushed against each other, something like electrical current surged through him. She shot him a mischievous smile and edged closer until he felt her heat.

The act of painting became a fever as he shaped detail from raw impression. The woman accentuated these details *chiaroscuro*, adding heavy shadowing to balance light and dark and bring out an impressive amount of depth. Her full breast pressed against his side as she leaned in. She was left-handed, allowing them to work together as a single entity, like some male-female chimera. She didn't wear a wedding ring. He didn't speak Italian, nor she English, but they were conversing as they created, both with their bodies and in the language of art. Their creation burned off the world and its cares—the global war, the dash to Delilah to haul out the injured loader, the shame and elation of machine-gunning German grenadiers in the dark, the long fight ahead.

His torso still tingling, Payne selected a slimmer brush and began the finer detail work. The woman stepped back to open a package of cigarettes and light one. Even now, he was still intensely aware of her, this Sicilian he'd only glanced at but who was striking him as the sexiest woman he'd ever met. On the canvas, the town stood in silent toil, the primordial hill looming over it under a free sky, filled with tension. On this hill, he slashed the columns of the ancient temple and a single, solitary figure making the climb to visit a foreign past.

It was a romantic vision, one that reminded him of Shelley's poem: "*And on the pedestal, these words appear: My name is Ozymandias, King of Kings; Look on my works, ye mighty, and despair!*" Man should brood on time and the fleeting nature of greatness and power and even existence, he thought, and in so doing make his eating, drinking, and merriment all the richer for it. "*Round the decay of that colossal wreck, boundless and bare. The lone and level sands stretch far away.*" Soon, time would bury all the statues of Mussolini, leader of fascism and founder of the empire, in the sands of history.

At last, Payne wiped the sweat from his forehead with his sleeve and paused, brush in hand, eyes roaming for the final detail. He found it with a single tiny stroke and took a step back to admire their work.

As if they were old friends, the woman leaned on his shoulder. She took a swig from her pitcher and passed it to him. "*Na lingua sula mai abbasta*, hmm?"

The truck honked in the main square. He drank thirstily from the pitcher and returned it. "Thank you. *Grazie*."

The war, which had granted him this brief respite, wanted him back.

Russo sat behind the wheel of the truck and started the engine. Wade hurried across the square and climbed into the seat beside him. Payne and Swanson hopped onto the back among the crates of wine.

"Looks like you found what you needed," Wade said.

Russo released the clutch and pressured the pedal. "I did indeed, Sergeant. I met the girl of my dreams."

"I saw her first," Swanson growled.

He chuckled at besting the loader. "Her father gave me permission to come back and court her. Apparently, he's a very wealthy and powerful man in these parts."

"Ducky for you, Mac."

"I'll make it up to you, Animal. I got the *vino* for the colonel but, for us, something even better. Herbs and garlic."

"A big ol' bag of stinky onions," the loader sulked.

"You'll thank me later when I spice up your meat hash with some oregano and garlic." Russo interpreted Swanson's silence as interest; the way to the loader's heart was through his stomach. He next shot Wade a questioning look. "How about you? Any good souvenirs?"

"I toured the ruins of a Roman temple. I think it was dedicated to Concordia, the goddess of marriage and agreements."

"Another good omen," Russo murmured.

He could barely focus on his driving. By the end of his deal with Signore Scicolone, he had felt like another transaction had completed. His head swirled with little memories. Her coy glance, her slight smile, the flash of scarlet petticoat.

Ignazia. She was the one.

"I met a woman," Payne said. "She painted something on my arm. Candelora?"

"That's her name."

"Candelora," the bog said, savoring it. Then he read the sentence she'd written on his arm. "What's it mean?"

Russo smiled. "It means, *find me.*"

Wade whistled. "You're a lucky dog, Leonard."

"I guess I am. Wait—what does, *na lingua sula mai abbasta* mean?"

"One language is never enough," Russo said.

Payne smiled. "She was really something. We didn't ... you know. We made a painting together."

The gunner guffawed. "I think you found the right girl for you."

"She let me take her picture. I gave her the painting."

"Everybody got lucky except me and the Professor, looks like," Swanson complained. "'Thousands of women,' the man says. 'Thousands of women feeling sexy while all their men have been gone for years.' Wasted trip."

"Wasn't wasted for me," Wade said. "I got plenty lucky. I got to see the kind of place I'd only been able to read about in books."

"Bunch of stones, no different than the ones we saw in Africa."

"Ancient ruins are like women, Animal. Each is beautiful in a different way and worth getting to know."

"So all I got out of this trip is better-tasting meat hash," the loader grumbled.

Russo passed back a bottle of wine. "And this fine *vino*, Animal. Cheer up and enjoy your hash. We could all be dead tomorrow."

CHAPTER FOURTEEN

PALERMO OR BUST

Tank Sergeant Wade read Shakespeare while Dog rumbled southwest toward a new assembly area outside Agrigento, which the 3rd Infantry Division had taken by assault after Patton finally gave the order to unleash the beast.

No longer would Seventh Army twiddle its thumbs playing flank guard to the Brits' glory drive. The entire army was on the move in western Sicily. 2nd Armored would claim the prize: Palermo, the Sicilian capital.

"*Fire answers fire,*" Wade read aloud. "*And through their paly flames, each battle sees the other's umbered face.*"

"What's that you're reading?" Swanson said.

"*Henry V* is a play about the British king and the events leading up to and after the Battle of Agincourt, during the Hundred Years' War."

The loader snorted. "Who would want to fight a hundred years?"

Wade read: "*Steed threatens steed, in high and boastful neighs piercing the night's dull ear; and from the tents the armorers, accomplishing the knights, with busy hammers closing rivets up, give dreadful note of preparation.*"

"Rivets, huh. Sounds like us. We're like the knights."

"Henry's army was sick, outnumbered, and low in morale. The French had plenty of knights and confidence. Heavy rains had made the ground poor for a charge on horse, though, and the English had the pike and the longbow."

"Also us," Swanson noted. "Except we seem to be the French. The English could easily be ginzos with antitank guns. Instead of mud, we got these narrow roads bottlenecking us."

The 15th Panzergrenadiers had vanished over the past week, presumably shifted east to face the British, who were closer to Messina. That still left the Assietta and Aosta Divisions opposing Seventh Army in western Sicily.

"Henry roused his men with a speech telling them God was on their side, they were all brothers in arms, and that their victory would make history. The battle completes his story of growing from a wild teenager into a great king."

"Sounds like Henry sold them a bunch of bullshit so they'd die for him being able to get more land and money."

Wade smirked, thinking, *I'll make a literary critic out of you yet, Animal.* "That's one way of looking at it."

"Them kings was a bunch of fascists themselves," Swanson growled. "Telling everybody to do and die for them. It's a stupid story."

Wade shrugged and returned to the text. A drop of sweat trickled down his nose and fell onto the page.

"Hey, Professor."

Wade steeled himself for another fart made all the

more sulfurous by the garlic Russo had added to their diet. "What's that?"

"Read a little more," the loader said.

Wade smiled. "*The poor condemned English, like sacrifices, by their watchful fires sit patiently and inly ruminate the morning's danger...*"

Recon Company led the way and did most of the fighting, followed by the Destroyers as usual, who'd acquired a reputation during this campaign as bloodthirsty killers and, therefore, received an honored place at the front of the main body. *The better you survived, the more the brass tried to kill you*, Corporal Swanson thought.

Otherwise, he didn't do much thinking as the column ground along the coastal highway toward Castelvetrano. His hatch open, he slumped over the .50, chin resting on the barrel. Fascist villas lined the northern overlook. Ahead, fresh smoke plumes marked ammo dumps the retreating Italians had destroyed.

The tanks passed donkeys, gutted by artillery fire and lying in a ditch. A row of dead Italian soldiers in blue-green uniforms. An M5 with its tracks blown off by an antitank mine. A farmer leading a horse-drawn cart and shouting, *I kiss your hand!*

"Vote Democrat," Swanson yelled back and said into the interphone, "I hope we get there soon. We're running out of booze."

"Not to mention food," Wade said. "Christ, we could walk there faster."

"We're an hour out from Castelvetrano," Russo told them.

"I have a dumb question," Payne said. "What is a fascist, exactly?"

"They're the bad guys, goofus," Swanson enlightened him.

"I mean, where does the word *fascism* come from?"

"You have a dime?" Wade said.

"Yeah."

"On one side, you see a woman, right?"

"Looks like the god Mercury to me."

"It's Liberty," said the gunner. "On the other side, there is a bunch of wood rods with an axe-head on top, along with some olive branches. The bundle of rods and the axe-head are *fasces*. To the Romans, it was a symbol of power."

"*Fasces*," Swanson said. "Don't that mean *shit*?"

Standing on the rear deck, Russo peed onto the road. "That's *feces*."

"President Roosevelt says fascism is ownership of government by a person or private group," Wade added. "Mussolini says it's the next evolution of government, where the state supersedes classes and individuals. It's hyper nationalist, authoritarian, and warlike."

"They're Reds too," Ackley said.

"Since Hitler crushed the unions and jailed all the socialists and communists, I don't think that's true," Payne pointed out.

"Fascism is a form of capitalism that borrows from socialism so it can wage permanent war," Wade explained. "Mussolini was a socialist but rejected it because it didn't serve nationalism. Fascism is a right-wing ideology. On the left, I guess its counterpart would be Soviet-style communism. Stalinism."

"You mean our ally," Ackley pointed out.

Wade shrugged. "Whatever the propaganda says, the war isn't a nice, neat story. It's all pretty complicated."

"I like things simple, Professor," Swanson said. "The fascists are the bad guys. That's all we need to know."

The column rolled into Castelvetrano to the usual spectacle of beauty and poverty. The townsfolk lined the streets, yelling, "Hoorah, Roosevelt!" and "*Viva America!*" An old man offered to point out fascist officials in the crowd.

Swanson waved him off and held up a pack of Chesterfields. "*Vino!* Anybody want to sell me some *vino?*"

By the time Dog reached the far end of town, the loader had scored a treasure in wine flasks and a basket filled with eggs, fresh vegetables, almonds, and grapes. He turned to watch Castelvetrano recede in the column's dust.

The people living there certainly didn't seem like the bad guys. They reminded him of his own people back home, folks trying to scratch out a living while under the thumb of bureaucrats living in some far-off capital.

In the end, it didn't matter. He didn't need a story to get him through the war, and he had even less need for philosophy. As he'd told the new guy at the airfield, anything that helped him survive was good, and everything trying to kill him was bad. It was so simple even the Professor couldn't argue with it.

As long as he got through this war without becoming one of the bad guys, he'd be happy.

PFC Payne nudged the sticks forward while Ackley, head lolling, snored in the bog seat. Ahead, M4 medium tanks rumbled through the dark in a snaking line of blackout tail lights.

An explosion flashed in the distance, briefly silhouetting the hills that gave Sicily its spectacular views but made it a nightmare for tank warfare. The delayed booms tingled in Payne's chest. Recon Company was skirmishing again.

"*Accura,*" Russo hissed over the interphone. "*Statti!*"

Payne pulled back on the sticks. The column was stopping. "If you give me an order, say it in English."

They'd been driving without rest for nearly forty-eight hours, and they were all punchier than usual.

"Mac's going native," Swanson said.

"Sorry, Payne," Russo said. "I'm just tired. I'm seeing double."

"Then catch some shuteye," said the loader. "I'll take over a bit."

"I think I'll take you up on that." The commander dropped into the turret and switched places with Swanson.

"Check interphone," Swanson said into his handheld microphone. "Testing, testing. Come in, New Guy. Over."

"Please stop," Payne answered.

"It's nice and roomy up here in the cupola. I could get used to this."

"If you were the commander, I think I'd go native too. As in switch sides."

The loader chuckled. "Move out, pawn. March, march!"

The convoy had started moving again. Dog navigated a sloping decline then had to drop gear to climb a steep grade. These winnowing roads had been built for people and mules, not thirty-ton tanks.

Payne thought about Candelora, and his chest tingled again. Going native didn't sound like a bad idea at all. Sicily was backward and impoverished, but it offered a lifestyle that couldn't be beat. Take your time, appreciate the little things, and worship wine, women, song, and art.

Painting with her had made a huge impression on him. *Find me*, she'd written on his arm. If he survived this war, he'd do that. He wasn't like Russo, hoping to find a wife here. But he was curious about seeing her again. Curious to take his time, appreciate the little things, and see what happened next.

The sun rose over a column of Italian soldiers marching to Agrigento, singing and laughing under waving white handkerchiefs. They wore long-billed caps and shabby uniforms and carried everything they owned on their backs. Badly equipped and poorly trained, they were done with Mussolini and his war.

Unable to take prisoners, the regiment simply passed them down the line to let them become somebody else's problem. The Italians streamed past in an endless blue-green river, hoping for American C rations at the end of the road.

The column stopped again. Wade and Russo stirred and stretched aching muscles. Russo took his place in the cupola, shunting the loader back to his hatch. The gunner lit a stove in the turret to boil coffee and fry the last of their eggs. Payne eyed a group of Italian soldiers approaching the tank and wrapped his hand around the grip of his bow gun.

"Do you have any cigarettes?" one of the soldiers asked.

Payne tossed him what was left in his pack. They made a show of running the cigarettes under their noses to smell the tobacco before huddling to share a match.

"You guys seem to be happy to get out of the war," Payne said.

The soldier who spoke English grinned. "Agrigento is beautiful city. Americans promised food there for us."

"At least these ginzos get to eat," Swanson grumbled. As the supply lines stretched across the rugged terrain, it was hard enough just staying gassed.

"And you not cut off our balls," the soldier added. "Best of all."

The loader chuckled. "Who told you we was gonna cut off your family jewels?"

"Germans say this. They are all gone. Tried to take trucks. We fought them. Germans no good. Never happy, always look down on us. 'See here, *Italiener*. You must dig zee fighting hole vunn unt vunn-half meters deep *precisely*.'"

Swanson chuckled again. "These guys are all right."

"You're safe now, *paesan*," Russo said. "America is here."

The soldier held up his cigarette like a toast.

"Americans are very good. Germans call Americans 'Montgomery's Italians.' We are brothers."

Swanson stopped laughing. "Lord, even the Krauts think we stink."

Beeping at the Italians, a jeep pulled up alongside Dog, its three-star passenger standing ramrod straight and toking on a big Havana.

"What is this, some kind of peace conference?" Patton fumed. "Keep these prisoners moving!"

Russo saluted. "Wilco, General."

"Is your big boy gassed up?"

"We're good to go, sir."

"Then what is the whole regiment doing parked on this road?"

"I heard there's an obstacle up a ways," Russo answered. "A farmer trying to get his mule off a bridge."

"I'll get it off the bridge," Patton said. "Or I'll shoot the sumbitch myself. Keep moving. We've got them on the run!"

"Any word on provisions, General?" Payne said.

Patton glared at him. "There's plenty of food for the army in Palermo. You want to eat, then take the city."

With that, the general sped off in his jeep, which wove around the tanks toward the bridge.

Minutes later, they heard a gunshot, and the column started moving again.

Standing on a ridge, Corporal Russo and the other platoon commanders stood with Captain Ratliff and surveyed Palermo, their operation's final prize.

Surrounded by heath-clad mountains, the Sicilian

capital sprawled across the coastal plain. Orange terracotta buildings were stacked down the slope toward the glittering azure harbor, which was filled with ships half sunk or capsized by Allied planes. Useless against modern arms, sections of an ancient wall still girdled this city of half a million. Bombing had flattened large swathes of the city. Smoke poured into the air from a blown ammunition dump.

Russo lowered his binoculars. "That's a lot of city."

"This is where they'll make their last stand," Ratliff said. "We take Palermo, the western half of Sicily will be ours, and we'll have a new supply base."

"Yes, sir," the platoon commanders murmured.

Ratliff unfolded a map. Behind him, the regiment's tanks stood in rows along the crest.

"We'll leapfrog past Recon and push through to the harbor," he said. "Our sister companies will be on our flanks in support, then they'll enter the city on these secondary roads. Russo, your platoon will lead the way. I'll be right behind you."

"Got it."

"Work with the doughs. You run into antitank guns, the doughs dismount and take them out. You run into anything else, you blast it into tiny pieces."

The commanders cracked grins. "Yes, sir."

"Now see to your platoons, and mount up."

Russo swaggered off toward the tanks, where his platoon wolfed down chow and coffee. Butch, Cranston, and Butter met him at Dog.

"What's the word, Tony?" Cranston said.

He repeated Ratliff's orders. "We're going in first."

Butch tossed the remains of his coffee on the ground. "Again."

"So much for rotating units to the front," Cranston groused.

Russo puffed out his chest. "Men, I just wanted to say I know I'm only acting platoon commander, but I'm proud of the fighting spirit..."

The tank commanders had walked off barking orders to their crews except for Cranston, who stood lighting one of his stubby cigars.

The man waved his match and tossed it. "I'm sure it would have been a great speech." He grinned and offered his hand. "See you in Palermo, Tony."

Russo shook it. "Good luck, Mickey."

He returned to Dog and ordered his men to mount up. Ackley cranked the engine and climbed in to start the ignition. Among the heath and myrtle, tanks rumbled to life. Exhaust fogged the hazy afternoon air.

Russo checked his watch. Minutes to go. "Destroyers 2 Actual to all Destroyers 2, stand by to march on Dog." He switched his radio control box to INT. "This is it, men. I just wanted to say, in case the worst happens, that I'm—"

"Are we there yet?" Swanson said in the turret.

"Tell the captain," Ackley called out.

Russo pursed his lips. "Have it your way. Driver, stand by to move out."

A squad of armored infantry climbed Dog's sponsons to ride along. The sergeant smiled at Russo. "What's cooking?"

"We're going to take a city today, I guess."

"Time to earn all that money Uncle Sam's been giving us."

"Destroyers Actual to all Destroyers, stand by to roll," Ratliff said on the company frequency. "Second Platoon, take us out."

"Driver, move out," Russo ordered. "Loader, once we're back on the road, put a round of HE in the gun."

Dog growled toward Palermo on clanking tracks. They passed the hull-down vehicles of Recon Company. Then they were on their own.

He turned in the cupola and puffed out his chest in pride. If only mama could see him now, leading an attack into a massive city. Vehicle after vehicle, the entire company was stacked behind him, and behind that, the main body of the regiment.

Today, Dog was the tip of the spear, its loaded cannon aimed forward. Behind, the other tanks aimed their guns toward the flanks. Last time he'd done this at Oran, the French promptly surrendered, and he didn't have to shoot anything. He doubted they'd be as lucky this time. Palermo had too much strategic importance to the Allies as a supply base and to the Axis for Italian morale.

"Eyes sharp all around," Russo told the platoon.

The road plunged out of the mountains onto the coastal plain, cutting through a patchwork of vineyards, orchards, and farms before the cultivation gave way to buildings. Russo raised his binoculars again to study a distant hazel orchard then swiveled to the dark windows of a farmhouse. Nothing moved.

The road turned into a boulevard that curved

toward the waterfront. A medieval keep stood alone on a rubbled block. Bombs had ripped the next building's facade clean off, exposing intact, furnished rooms like a giant dollhouse. Over the tank engines, he heard cheering from the piazza ahead.

Russo laughed. "I'll be damned." He switched the radio to the company frequency. "Destroyers 2 to Destroyers Actual."

"Go ahead, Destroyers 2," Ratliff said. "What have you got?"

"The locals are having a party ahead of us. I think the city is surrendering."

"Roger that, Destroyers 2. I'll pass it up."

While he did that, Russo passed down the word to his tank commanders. Second Platoon rolled along the boulevard and straight into a victory parade. White sheets and homemade American flags hung from every window surrounding the piazza, which was filled with thousands of cheering people. The tanks waded into the crowds to a shower of flower petals and lemons.

Children gaped at the tanks. Old men raised canvas wine flasks in scores of toasts. Some threw the stiff-armed fascist salute. Women blew kisses to the blushing tankers and offered handfuls of almonds. On the far side of the square, Italian soldiers stood in awkward ranks, waiting to surrender.

The celebration was made all the sweeter by its surprise. He'd expected mines, antitank guns, and snipers in windows, not this bloodless victory. The Italian army had fled from the path of America's armored might.

Palermo was theirs without firing a single shot.

Russo beamed at it all. "I feel like Julius Caesar." He flung his hands out with fingers extended in V's for victory. "I came, I saw, I conquered!"

At the center of the piazza, a mob looped a rope around the neck of a statue of Mussolini, and they pulled it down with a crash to wild cheering.

"Nice entrance!" someone in the crowd said. "What took you tread heads so long?"

"Driver, stop!" Russo looked down and found a smirking infantryman raising a pitcher of wine to toast 2nd Armored's arrival. "Who the hell are you?"

"We're 3rd Infantry Division. Welcome to Palermo!"

CHAPTER FIFTEEN

OCCUPATION

PFC Payne set up his easel on a hilltop overlooking the ancient chapel and the regimental bivouac. He breathed deeply and took in the picturesque coastal town of Carini to the north and the glittering Mediterranean behind it.

Another beautiful day in Sicily.

Palermo sprawled to the east. There, engineers toiled to repair the port and rail systems and make the city a base for further operations. The Germans had ground down the British Eighth Army on the approaches to Mount Etna, and now Montgomery needed help from the Americans he'd cast aside.

Seventh Army marched east toward Messina. Out for glory, Patton and Montgomery were eager to stick a finger in the other's eye. The race was on.

But not 2nd Armored. Their race was over.

No longer the spearhead, the division had become an occupation force. Command peeled units off to maintain order in distant towns where looters, prisoners, and local governments needed attention.

In recognition of how hard Destroyer Company had fought, the brass allowed it to rest, though that wouldn't last long. There was far more wait than hurry in war, but the Army knew how to fill the waiting with busywork.

Payne mounted his stretched canvas on the easel and laid out his paints, which he'd acquired in Palermo and kept in a satchel. Then from the pocket of his tanker overalls, he removed the handful of photographic prints, which he'd paid a photographer to develop.

The images showed a dead Tiger against a smoky backdrop, German prisoners marching smartly on Oran's sunny docks, Payne's crew grinning in front of Dog in Morocco. He lingered on a photograph of Candelora, hand on her hip, turning to give him a mischievous smile under a mop of black curls.

He smiled back and thought, *Ciau, woman.*

Find me, he heard her say.

Payne returned the photograph to his pocket and set a different one at the bottom-right corner of his blank canvas. In the black-and-white image, Sergeant Wade sat on Moroccan dirt with his back against Dog's dusty tracks, an Oh Henry! bar in one hand and *Henry V* in the other.

He'd paint this and give it to the gunner as a gift. The photo he'd keep.

Thinking of Candelora now, he decided to use the wet-on-wet technique again for speed. He squeezed his paint tubes onto his metal tray, a lid torn off a .30 ammo box. Selecting a large brush, he blocked out Wade, the tank treads, the brown earth. Then he layered his details, light and shadow, selecting finer and finer brushes and mixing pigments when needed.

At last, he stepped back with a smile.

"Is that Wade?" a familiar voice said.

He turned to find Russo admiring the painting.

Payne rubbed his hands with a rag. "Yup."

"It's good. You're really good with a brush, *goombah*."

"I'm happy to be able to work again." He'd treated his homesickness by bringing home to him.

"Looks like that dame in Campobello inspired you a little, huh?"

Payne chuckled. "I guess she did."

The tank commander cracked a grin. "How'd you like to see her again?"

Corporal Russo handed Payne the Tommy gun and started the jeep, which growled out of the motor pool and into the cedars. He sang a Sicilian love song as the jeep cleared the forest and roared down the sun-washed road.

It had taken 2nd Armored two weeks to help secure the beachhead and fight its way to Palermo. Barring accidents on the road, diehard partisans, and German snipers, the fifty-mile return trip would take a day.

They passed fields of melons, tomatoes, and garlic. Farmers tended these crops as they had for thousands of years. A falcon traced a lazy circle in the bright sky over the southern hills.

"It's a different way of life out here," Payne said.

"No kidding," Russo agreed. "A man could get used to the pace."

He'd never emigrate, which would mean leaving his family back home. Instead, he pictured becoming a great man living in both countries. He and Ignazia would live in America but frequent their Sicilian villa.

Yes, he could picture it.

"What's next for us, do you think?"

"Patrolling."

In two days, the company would roll to Alcamo, another coastal town southwest of Carini, and set up an outpost. There, they'd patrol and guard key locations. And search for weapons. Sicily was now a junkyard of weaponry just lying around along with unexploded ordnance and booby traps.

"I mean after that. Is this it for us?"

"We've done our share. I think we've earned a trip back home and a nice parade." Russo could picture that too.

"Wade says we're invading mainland Italy next."

"He's often right, but not always. You worried about it?"

Payne shook his head. "I don't want to go home yet. My war only lasted two weeks. I'd like to see this thing through. When Hitler's gone, I'll be done."

"Well," said Russo. "I'm sure it could be arranged. Aren't you homesick?"

"If I tell you something, will you promise not to laugh?"

"Sure."

"All this?" Payne gestured around him. "I'm actually having fun."

Russo did laugh, but not at Payne. He laughed because it was true.

"The killing is horrific," the bog went on. "I *hate* the killing. But the travel and sights. The experiences. And hell, sending a shell downrange and seeing it blow something up? It's crazy to say it, but it's...beautiful."

"I think every tanker understands how you feel," Russo said. "Don't get me wrong, though. I'd rather be home making money and marrying a gorgeous girl than driving around with the likes of Animal and Ack-Ack, getting shot at."

As they approached a supply convoy, he stopped talking to focus on his driving. Payne hailed the honking truckers as Russo weaved in and out of their formation. A glance at the sky told him it'd be dark soon, so they stopped at a captured Italian depot to stay the night.

The next morning, they drove into Campobello, which a platoon peeled from the 26th Infantry Regiment now guarded. No MPs, however, which boded well for their plans to break the rules by fraternizing with Sicilian girls.

Russo frowned at a pair of patrolling riflemen. "I doubt we'll be able to do any good trading. These vultures probably picked the place clean."

Payne got out and slung his Tommy over his shoulder. "That's not what we came for anyway."

"You got that right," Russo grinned and sang, "*T'amu, ti vogghiu, m'ammanchi!*"

The piazza was busy with townspeople going about their errands but was otherwise empty; they'd missed market day in any case. Women filled the air with loud chatter as they walked past hauling water and firewood. At the edge of the square, a gang of old men seated at a table shared a wine flask.

Payne led him down a street and up a hill into a garden, where they found a woman in a shabby sundress painting at an easel in the shade of a lemon tree, hand on her hip. She was a stunner; the bog had an eye for beauty.

She smiled at the approaching tankers and called out to them.

"What'd she say?" Payne asked him.

"She said, 'You found me.'"

Payne and Candelora stared at each other for a while. Russo fidgeted in the mounting animal tension, feeling very much a third wheel. Finally, she held out her hand and spoke again.

Russo grinned. "She said—"

Payne held up his hand. "Thanks, Tony. I got it from here."

The woman took that hand and led him into her house. Russo walked away still grinning. What a lucky bastard.

Now it was his turn. He passed orange terracotta building facades until he found the store. The door was boarded up.

"Are you looking for Signore Scicolone?" said a female voice.

Russo turned to take in a woman smirking at him with a jug of water perched on her head. "Yes. Where is he?"

"The Americans took him. He's a fascist." She spat on the cobblestones.

"Can you point me to his house?"

The woman gave him directions. "You should go back where you came from while you're still a happy man."

"*Grazij.*" Ignoring her ominous advice, he ran the entire way, his heart pounding with worry.

Ignazia was alone now, possibly ostracized and even in danger. Russo would have to step up. He'd give her cigarettes and invasion scrip to help her get by until he could return to properly take care of her. He wouldn't be able to protect her, however. He'd have to figure out a way.

Russo skidded to a halt.

A beautiful woman was walking toward him. It was Ignazia, but a different Ignazia now, her long curls freed from their bun, her shawl tied around her neck like a scarf to expose tan shoulders, her laughter filling the air.

She strolled arm in arm with a tall infantry lieutenant, as young and handsome as anybody Hollywood would cast for the role. Engrossed in each other, they didn't even notice him as they passed. With a final flash of scarlet petticoat under her black skirt, she was gone.

Ignazia had found her own way, it seemed.

Russo sagged, feeling sorry for himself, then jumped back as two women ran past shouting, a gaggle of children in their wake. Other people hurried after them shaking their fists with happy cries. Russo trailed them back to the piazza, which was filling with townspeople. An old man with tears in his eyes grabbed his hand and enthusiastically shook it. A heavyset matron thanked him and planted kisses on both of his cheeks.

"You're welcome," he answered between smooches. "What's going on?"

"Mussolini," the matron cried.

"Mussolini, Mussolini!" the old man joined in. He made a fist and chopped the crook of his arm with his other hand. "The tyrant is gone!"

They told him the Italian king and ruling fascist council had deposed and arrested the dictator. Italy would no doubt surrender soon, they said, and join the Allies in their fight against Germany.

The townsfolk crowded around to show their gratitude. Sicily wasn't his country, but these were his people. Every handshake, every hug and kiss, every Â *saluti!* and *Viva* America! made all the fighting feel worthwhile.

His grief for a lost love slipped away as another type of love buoyed him.

With his German prisoner in the backseat, Tank Sergeant Wade drove his jeep around a crater in the road and continued on his return to Alcamo.

During the two months of occupation duty, this was as exciting as things got. Patton beat Montgomery to Messina in the middle of August, though the tankers had been preoccupied at the time with a downpour that had flooded their tent and forced them to sleep on ammo boxes. Seventh Army ceased to exist as a combat formation, its units reorganized. In September, the Allies invaded mainland Italy. In response, the Germans occupied the northern half of the peninsular country and put Mussolini back in charge of a new puppet state.

Through it all, Destroyer Company patrolled a

dusty corner of Sicily.

Thompson in his lap, Swanson smoked a Chesterfield in the seat beside him. "I think they forgot all about us. We ain't that different than this Kraut."

The loader turned and leered at the emaciated grenadier, who sat shaking with hunger and fatigue. The soldier had finally had enough and walked into the nearest village to surrender, which set the locals scurrying to the Americans for the reward. Wade wondered how the man had survived so long on his own, waiting for his division to return to reclaim Sicily.

"I wish he spoke English," Wade said.

Swanson gave the grenadier a cigarette and turned back. "Why?"

"I don't know. Lots of reasons. I could find out why he's fighting, maybe."

"Again, why?"

"*Vielen dank*," the German rasped after taking his first drag.

Swanson smirked. "Did you hear that, Professor? He said his name is Weiss. He acts all superior and likes to read books and he's a real pain in the ass to the other grunts, who ditched him in Sicily."

"You heard him wrong," Wade said. "His name is actually Switzer. He hates everybody but can't shut up and keep it to himself, so he made his entire platoon miserable. They were happy to get shot."

Swanson chuckled. "Feel better knowing your enemy?"

"It's natural to be curious what motivates men who are trying to kill me."

"And it's natural not to want to know men I'm trying to kill."

Wade shrugged. "I see your point."

"Ha! I thought you was supposed to be the smart one."

"I mean I see your point that this guy is just like us," he said. "Just like you, specifically. It makes them far easier to blow up."

The jeep passed a truck that had tipped over and was surrounded by infantrymen trying to right it. Stuck in Sicily. At first, Wade had hated it and wanted to keep moving. The sooner the Germans lost, the sooner he could go home.

Then he'd received a response to his V-mail, another letter from Alice. It read she was happy he wrote back. Happy he still loved and wanted her. The letter smelled like her perfume and was filled with hopes and promises for a happy future.

That letter killed any desire he had to get back into the war because it suddenly became far more important to make sure he stayed alive until its end. When combat operations ended in Sicily mid-August, he was happy. When the Allies invaded southern Italy without him, he was even happier.

Maybe he was making a mistake taking her back, maybe not. He did love her, which he supposed settled it for him. For now, it was easy to imagine everything being perfect when he got back home.

Easier to imagine going home at all.

He sensed a truth about life and death, which was you had to take life for granted to live it. Thinking about death made it all seem pointless.

Wade drove into the camp, turned the prisoner over to the MPs, and returned the jeep to the motor pool. The moment he saw Russo's face, he knew right away something was wrong.

"Ackley broke his fingers," the commander said.

Swanson guffawed. "In the hatch?"

"Yup."

Wade could only shake his head. "How?"

"He skipped out on duty and snuck into Dog for a nap. When he was closing the main hatch, he mashed his fingers."

"Serves him right," Swanson crowed. "Dumbass."

"It leaves us short." Wade sighed and slung his Thompson over his shoulder. "I guess I'll sign the jeep out again and drive over to Carini for a replacement."

Breaking in a new guy would be difficult, especially considering most of their time was spent on occupation duties and very little on training.

Swanson was still laughing. "This is one of those situations where both sides get something, you know, where—"

"A win-win," Wade filled in, used to playing the loader's dictionary by now.

"Ol' Ack-Ack gets out of the war for a while, and we get him out of our hair. I'd say we got the better end of that stick."

Wade and Russo exchanged smiles. Swanson was right; nobody would miss Ackley. With him, it had been like sharing a tank with a five-year-old version of Swanson.

"I know I'm not going to miss seeing meat and beans plastered on his face," Wade said. "You coming, Animal?"

The loader shrugged. "Sure, why not."

The drive to Carini was uneventful. The tankers stepped out of the jeep and found the repple-depple filled with bored recruits. In the administrative tent, the master sergeant sat with his feet on a table, catching up on the real world with a copy of *Life* magazine.

"Hey, Sergeant," Wade said. "We need an M4 bow gunner."

The man didn't look up. "Then go fetch one, and bring him here."

"How about I fetch one from the roster?"

Exasperated at the interruption, the sergeant made a show of setting his magazine down and planting his boots on the ground. He reached for the clipboard on the table and slid it across for Wade to take a look.

Then he returned to his magazine.

Wade perused the names, which meant nothing to him, and the men's qualifications, which did. He nudged Swanson. "I think we know this guy."

The loader chuckled. "Eight Ball."

"We'll take this man," Wade told the master sergeant. "Eugene W. Clay."

Tall and gangly as they remembered, Clay showed up minutes later toting his barracks bag. "It's about time!"

The men shook hands. Swanson even smiled at the reunion.

"It's really good to see you alive and in one piece,"

Wade said.

"As soon as I started to feel right again, I asked to rejoin my outfit," Clay told him. "I was scared, if I waited too long, they'd send me somewhere else. Sure enough, the adjutant wanted to send me to 1st Armored in Italy. I kept saying no and bugging him until he finally sent me here to shut me up."

"Good to know that works," Swanson said, already back to his old self.

Wade grinned at the man who'd saved his life. "Come on, Eugene. We have a lot of catching up to do."

CHAPTER SIXTEEN

CONGRATULATIONS

The tankers gathered around Dog to say goodbye. Barracks bags at their feet and musettes over their shoulders, they took a final look at the big vehicle that for months they'd called home.

Long miles of road marching had worn it out. Machine guns and shrapnel had scored and scarred its metal skin. The smoking bulldog grinned on the turret. A row of German crosses under it bragged of kills. Dried mud clumped around the bogies.

Corporal Swanson patted the warm hull. "Good Dog."

After driving Dog back to Carini, they'd gotten the tank ready to turn in to the supply unit. Its crew was finally leaving Sicily.

The next time they saw their tank, it would have a fresh paint job and overhauled engine. Assuming they got the same vehicle for the next operation.

Assuming they weren't going back to the real world.

"Think it's the last time?" Clay said.

"We did our part," Russo said. "They're sending us home."

Clay was shaking. "I was hoping to get back into the fight."

"You should have stayed in the hospital," Swanson growled at him. The skinny kid was either still recovering or had a bad case of battle stress.

"I was going to end up in another unit. I feel safer with you guys."

"Yeah, you'll feel real safe when we're under fire again, numbnuts." The whole thing made him angry, mostly because he felt the same way, though he was the kind of guy who hated the idea of depending on anybody except himself.

"What do you think, Wade?" Russo said.

"Uncle Sam spent a lot of money on us," the gunner said. "The Army owns us. We're going to Italy or England."

Russo shook his head in disbelief. In his mind, no doubt, he'd earned his discharge. If the Army kept him in the fight, it would feel like Uncle Sam was using him until he got killed.

Swanson could relate. But while he usually scoffed at the Professor's gloomy predictions, this time he kept his mouth shut. Wade had it right this time. The Army wasn't going to send home experienced tankers until they rolled into Berlin, and until then, the big green machine sure as hell didn't care about Russo's feelings.

The company staff sergeant called the Destroyers to fall in. The tankers formed ranks in front of their vehicles, which stood parked in neat rows with guns leveled.

Captain Ratliff glowered at them all with tough love. "It's been an honor!"

The staff sergeant yelled at them to fall out and mount the trucks that would drive them to the harbor. The tankers cheered and grabbed their bags.

"See that, *Duce*?" Swanson said. "That's how you give a speech."

The crew mounted its designated deuce-and-a-half, which it shared with the rest of the platoon, including Lieutenant Pierce, who'd returned from sick leave just in time to rejoin his unit. Hugging their barracks bags, the men crammed in like sardines. They were a cheerful bunch, having won a quick campaign with few losses and believing they were all heading stateside.

"First thing when I get home, I'm gonna sleep in a real bed," Russo said. "For about two weeks straight. What about you, Eugene?"

"I don't know," Clay said. "I guess I'll go to the lake, find a nice tree to sit under, and just be alive. Just breathe for a while."

"When I get home, I'm going to patch things up with Alice." Wade glared at the loader as if expecting him to ruin it.

Swanson preferred playing with his mice instead of rending them limb from limb. "I got nothing against that, Professor. I actually wish you luck."

"What about you? What are you going to do when you get back?"

"Why would I think about that? Odds are, I'm not."

"Come on, Animal," Russo said. "You could at least play along."

"I'm just telling it like it is, Mac." The truth was Swanson didn't have much waiting for him back home, but he wasn't about to admit it.

"Fun-killer," Russo muttered.

"All right, I'm gonna screw my way across whatever

port we land. Happy?"

"Never mind. I'm sorry I asked you. What about you, Payne?"

The man smiled. "Nothing comes to mind. I guess I'll find out when I get there."

The trucks parked at the harbor. The tankers dismounted and went through the usual bureaucracy before crossing the gangplank to board the HMS *Poseidon*. They stowed their gear in their rooms on C deck and returned to line the main deck's gunwales in time for their departure.

The merchant ship blasted its horn and backed from the pier toward its waiting destroyer escorts, offering a final view of Sicily.

"*Salutamu*," Russo whispered in farewell.

The tankers stared at the receding island in a strangled silence. Swanson tore a page from Clay's book and just breathed.

Consisting of ships carrying both 2nd Armored and the 9th Infantry Division, the large convoy cruised across the Mediterranean Sea. Swanson spent his time in physical training, attending lectures about the danger of venereal disease, and hiding when the ship's chiefs picked men to volunteer for work.

Even with the daily regimen, the tankers returned to their favorite idle activities of scrapping and gambling and trading souvenirs. Otherwise, the trip was uneventful except for a few U-boat alerts and abandon-ship drills.

Arms draped over the railing, smoking one of his

Chesterfields, Swanson took in the view from the deck. Off the starboard bow, the Rock of Gibraltar loomed over the harbor and its floating guardians, a vast array of cruising destroyers and other ships. Ahead lay the Pillars of Hercules and the Atlantic Ocean.

All looking glum, his crewmates approached and leaned against the railing.

Swanson guffawed. "I told you, you idiots. Okay, let's hear it."

Wade held out a sheet of paper. "It's from General Eisenhower. Read it and weep."

He waved it off. "Read it to me, Professor."

"'Soldiers of 2nd Armored Division, I wish you a hearty congratulations,'" the gunner read. "'You have been selected to train in England as part of the Allied Expeditionary Force now preparing to invade Fortress Europe—'"

Swanson held up his hand again. "I got it. I told you idiots."

Wade folded the paper and pocketed it. "Yes, you did."

"Why are you down in the dumps, Prof? You knew it too."

The gunner shrugged. "A part of me was hoping."

"Then you're even dumber than these other mopes." Swanson leaned and spat into the foaming bow wake far below. "There ain't no hope out here."

Yet it persisted among these men, and no amount of armor in the world could protect against it. Hope was an 88 round fired at point-blank range.

Russo crumpled his sheet in his hand and tossed it

overboard. "He made it sound like we won the lottery. 'Congratulations,' he says. I'm not doing it."

Swanson jerked his thumb over his shoulder. "Then take a jump and swim to Morocco. Your choice, Mac."

The commander sagged against the railing. "Damn it. I can't win."

"There's only one way to win," Payne said.

"New Guy's right," Swanson said. "The only way we're going home alive and in one piece is to beat Hitler."

"Then that's what we'll hope for," the bog told him.

Swanson didn't respond. Hope was dangerous, but it also kept them going. Hope was its own kind of armor, the kind that didn't come with a tank, and, he thought, it might see them all the way to Berlin.

AFTERMATH

With the capture of Messina on August 17, 1943, the Allies completed the conquest of Sicily and secured the Mediterranean Sea. Operation Husky, which had started badly for the Allies, ended in success.

The collapse of Italian morale was a significant consequence of the operation. In February, the Soviet Army had destroyed the Italian expeditionary force participating in the German invasion. In May, Axis forces in North Africa had surrendered. The Allied invasion of Sicily was the last straw.

After Palermo fell, Mussolini was removed by a vote of no confidence by the Grand Council of Fascism and the Italian king, who secretly entered negotiations with the Allies to discuss terms of surrender. When an Allied army invaded mainland Italy in September, however, Germany occupied the country and put Mussolini back in power as head of a new puppet state.

While decisive, Operation Husky had its failures. The Allies allowed seventy thousand Italian troops and the bulk of the German forces to evacuate and fight another day. Dispersion of Allied troops across western Sicily surprised even the Germans, which begs the question of how the operation might have turned out if Montgomery had trusted his ally or did not object to Seventh Army landing in the northwest instead of at the southern beaches.

Nonetheless, America's top military leaders had gained additional valuable experience, while her soldiers proved themselves a capable adversary. Throughout most of the rest of the war, the Allies would have the initiative, launching a long, savage effort to destroy Nazi Germany.

The beginning of the end would occur in Normandy in June 1944.

WANT MORE?

Thank you for reading! If you enjoyed the second episode of *Armor*, please review the book on Amazon and be sure to check out the next book in the series.

You might also be interested in Craig's *Crash Dive* series, which depicts submarine warfare in the Pacific against the Empire of Japan during WW2. The series is available in Kindle eBook (both individually and as a box set), trade paperback, and audiobook.

Sign up for Craig's mailing list to stay up to date on new releases and receive a link to Craig's interactive submarine adventure, *Fire One*.

Learn more about Craig's writing at www. CraigDiLouie.com.

And turn the page to read the first chapter of *Armor III: Fortress Europe*!

THE STAGE:

OPERATION OVERLORD

The capture of Sicily in August 1943 triggered the collapse of the Italian war effort and secured the Mediterranean for Allied shipping. The September invasion of mainland Italy resulted in the *Wehrmacht* occupying the northern half of the country and contesting every yard with bullets and blood.

The Allies were now ready to liberate France, open a stronger second front in Western Europe to relieve pressure on the exhausted Soviet Union, and build a continental base for a long offensive straight to Berlin and the war's end.

Operation Overlord was born.

The invasion would begin with an assault across the English Channel to crack the Atlantic Wall and establish a beachhead in Fortress Europe. War planners chose France's Normandy region as an optimal landing site. In December 1943, President Roosevelt appointed General Dwight Eisenhower as supreme commander of the Allied Expeditionary Force.

By May 1944, nearly three million Allied troops had amassed in southern England. Meanwhile, more than five thousand ships and eight thousand planes stood ready to support the invasion. Juggling infighting, politics, and weather forecasts, Eisenhower set June 5 as D-Day, the invasion date. While Allied troops entered

Rome that day, achieving a major war milestone, bad weather forced Eisenhower to postpone the Normandy invasion until June 6.

On that day, 175,000 Allied troops boarded transports and planes for the largest seaborne invasion in history. Facing them in Normandy were eighty thousand Wehrmacht soldiers under the overall command of the Desert Fox himself, Field Marshal Erwin Rommel.

The resulting clash would be one of the war's fiercest battles and herald the beginning of the end for Nazi Germany.

D-DAY

CHAPTER ONE

INVASION

Salted with whitecaps, the English Channel flexed under a paling sky. Landing Craft, Tank (LCT) 188 bobbed on the dusky flood, part of a vast armada following glowing buoys laid by the trail-blazing minesweepers.

Yellow light haloed the southern horizon. Booms jarred the atmosphere and swept across the water. This was the heavy bombers, dropping their massive payloads. The Navy's big ships joined in with a deafening cannonade. The blasting guns flashed in the murk. The sun continued its inexorable rise.

H-Hour minus one.

The LCT's engines throbbed beneath the main deck, upon which the crews of four M4 medium tanks finished waterproofing their vehicles. At Tank #55, which its crew called Dog, Tank Sergeant Anthony Russo inspected the canvas flotation screen girdling his vehicle's armor and hoped it would work today.

"Hurry it up," he shouted at his crew over the strong southeasterly wind.

Water sprayed the already drenched tankers as the flat-bottomed landing craft rolled into another alarming list. Private Payne coughed into a barf bag.

"Happy D-Day, Herr Hitler, Happy D-Day to you!" Sergeant Cranston sang from Duck Soup.

Sergeant Wade winced from seasickness. "What's the plan, Tony?"

"What do you mean? We're invading France!"

Dog was among the tanks chosen to lead the first wave onto the beach, commanded by Russo, newly minted as a tank sergeant in recognition of his service in the successful Sicilian operation.

"I meant, how are we getting ashore? We can't swim in this chop!"

Ahead lay a five-mile stretch of coast designated as Omaha Beach. At high tide, one to two hundred yards of flat stretched beyond the shingle embankment and seawall and rose to steep bluffs fortified with bunkers and pillboxes.

Only they weren't attacking at high tide. The problem was numerous obstacles riddled the beach: hedgehogs constructed of crossed steel beams, log posts and ramps rigged with mines, Belgian gates. The first assault wave would go in at half flood, when low tide exposed these obstacles across an extra three hundred yards of ground. Once cleared, the next wave could land closer to the bluffs and their five narrow wooded valleys providing paths to the interior.

After the tanks hit the beach, they would suppress enemy positions, but the problem was delivering them to the shore under fire and in potentially deep water. In response, the British developed an amphibious retrofit: the DD tank, which stood for *Duplex Drive* but the tankers called *Donald Ducks*.

Dog now featured a rubberized canvas skirt, which was inflatable using compressed air tanks and supported by metal hoops and struts. Vertical stacks would keep the air intake and exhaust high and dry. The tank's modified transmission allowed the driver to deliver power from the rear sprocket wheels to twin bronze propellers affixed to the rear engine compartment, enabling a sailing speed up to four knots.

Today, Dog would become a thirty-ton boat.

During their months-long stay in the United Kingdom, Russo and his crew had trained on their DD at Fritton Lake and in the waters surrounding the Isle of Wight. The flotation worked for the most part but only if the water was calm.

In rough seas, the tanks sank to the bottom. In April, the Americans and British had conducted a live D-Day rehearsal in Studland. Due to choppy waters, several Valentine DD tanks went under and dragged six men down with them.

"These Coast Guard guys know what we can and can't do," Russo told Wade. "The captain won't launch us if he doesn't think we'll make it. He'll drive us straight up to the beach. Lieutenant Pierce himself assured me of this."

Already pale, the gunner whitened further. "If you say so."

"The invasion won't succeed if the doughs don't clear the obstacles. The doughs need us to cover them while they do that. The whole thing depends on us getting ashore. Our own side isn't going to try to kill us along the way."

Wade shrugged. Always the pessimist, he wasn't buying it.

Russo steadied his landlubber legs and returned to work finishing Dog's waterproofing, taping up the gun barrel. As long as he kept busy, he could hold off vomiting. They hadn't even begun to fight, and already they were cold, drenched, cranky, and worn out. Only Corporal Clay, who had some sailing experience, was holding it together without losing his battle breakfast.

"Now hear this! Now hear this!" the loudspeakers blared. "Tankers, man your tanks! Tankers, man your tanks!"

Lieutenant Pierce staggered across the rolling deck. "This is it. Second Platoon, mount up!"

Russo waved at him. "Lieutenant! How far are we from shore?"

He'd accept a thousand yards, maybe two. Any farther than that in this rough sea and they were goners.

"Six thousand yards."

He glared up at the wheelhouse towering aft over the main deck then back at the platoon commander. "What the hell, Lieutenant?"

"Everybody's launching, Sergeant," Pierce said coolly. "Everybody goes. That means we go. So get your tank ready."

Russo turned to tell Wade, who nodded and said, "Told you so."

The plan called for the swimming tanks to disembark at five to six thousand yards, and that's what the LCT's captain would do. No more, no less.

Or so the skipper said. Russo wondered if the man simply didn't want to go any closer to the shore out of fear of being sunk.

It didn't matter. Orders were orders. "We can do this."

Corporal Swanson opened the nozzle on the air

tank strapped to the front plate. "Another day in the Army, Mac. Sending the gullible to do the suicidal."

"Where's your life jacket?"

"On the turret, where it'll be when we sink. I can't fit through the hatch if I'm wearing that stupid thing."

"You'll be up top with me then. Wade will stay in the turret."

"First good idea you've had yet, Mac."

"Grab a pair of binoculars. You'll be my eyes while I'm driving."

High-pressure air hissed through tubing into the canvas skirt, which began to inflate. Payne and Clay mounted the rear deck and raised the supports to hold the flotation screen upright.

No matter how many times Russo did this, he couldn't help but stare in dread at how flimsy the whole thing looked. Most of the tank would submerge during the trip; only a foot of freeboard would be above water. Rough seas could spill over the top, flood the engine, tear the flotation screen apart. The sizable waves already threatened to capsize the LCT; Dog would surely sink.

"Not today," he thought aloud, in full Sicilian-Superman mode. He hadn't fought through North Africa and Sicily, hadn't trained for months in dreary, soggy England, only to drown on France's doorstep. He was going to make it.

The screen inflated to form a canvas box around the tank. Dog looked like a giant basket on tracks now.

Cocky veterans of Sicily, the platoon erupted with a martial shout as they clambered onto their armored vehicles and dropped into their stations. Russo felt a twinge of embarrassment as his own sulking crew moped their way into Dog. He mounted last to stand on a platform behind the turret, where he took hold of the grab bar and vertical lever serving as a tiller.

The radio blatted. "Platoon, start your engines!"

Dog roared and settled into a steady rumble. Exhaust fogged above the tanks, and the sea wind swept it away.

"Now hear this! Now hear this!" the loudspeakers called. "Tankers, thirty seconds to disembark! Thirty seconds! God be with you."

"Men," Russo addressed his crew over the interphone and caught himself. No speeches, not now. "Good luck."

"'Where were you, Grandpa, on D-Day?'" Swanson said in a spot-on imitation of General Patton's high-pitched snarl. "'Well, boy, I was swimming.'"

Nobody laughed. The men were too cold, wet, seasick, and no doubt preoccupied with trying to remember the evacuation procedures and how to use the Davis submerged escape apparatus.

"On the plus side," Russo said, "this is probably the last time we'll be attacking from a landing craft. Nothing but land between Normandy and—"

The whistle blew. Ahead, the ramp splashed down. Normally fitting nine tanks, the LCT carried only four of the bulkier DDs. Pierce led the way in his Delilah, followed by Democracy, Duck Soup, and Dog.

Duck Soup started to edge across the hold.

"Driver, move out on Duck Soup," Russo said. "Stand by for the props."

"Roger," Payne said.

Delilah and Democracy were already foundering in

the swell. Duck Soup rolled into the water next.

Swanson scanned the sea with his binoculars. "Democracy is going down."

Too late to back out now. "Driver, keep going!"

This was the hardest part of swimming—rolling off the ramp into the sea in just the right way without going belly up and sinking like a stone. Russo gripped his handhold to brace for the splash.

"Alley oop," the loader said.

Dog crashed into the water with an alarming wobble. The wind swept away the exhaust and replaced it with the sea's briny smell.

"Driver, engage the props," Russo said.

"Engaging!"

The propellers began to churn water. The floating tank puttered forward. Russo glanced at Democracy's crew deploying an inflatable raft from their sinking DD. Their flotation screen had buckled, and the waves had spilled over the freeboard and flooded the engine.

"That's what they get for not checking the struts," Swanson said.

"Or the struts couldn't handle the strain," Russo said.

He eyed his own screen with worry. A mere three-foot-high wall of canvas kept the entire ocean at bay. Whatever he'd told Wade, he was done trusting that the brass knew what it was doing and that their plans would always work. Russo was just one dot on a huge number of dice being cast in a life-or-death gamble. If he made it ashore, he made it. If he didn't, nobody would care.

All around him, the sea flexed like a powerful and living thing impervious to all of man's carefully laid plans. Puffing exhaust from their vertical stacks, the rest of the DDs, some thirty in all, battled the flood to cross to the Normandy coast three miles away. The Navy's big guns crashed. Shells howled overhead.

Following in Delilah's wake, Dog paddled across the whitecaps at a sluggish couple of knots. Crowned with drifting smoke and dust from the bombardment, the coastal bluffs seemed impossibly distant. The English Channel hissed and sprayed into his eyes. Russo was soaked to the bone now and shivering in the wind.

Swanson cackled. "Another tank's going down."

"Eyes forward, Animal! You're supposed to be watching the beach."

The loader shrugged. "Have it your way."

"And why are you laughing?"

"Because this whole thing is nuts. Some real salutin'-the-angels shit."

"Once we get to the beach, we'll need to take down the skirt and have a target ready to shoot at."

"I love your, your—when the glass is half full—"

"Optimism," Wade shouted in the turret, his voice edged with panic.

"Yup. Your optimism, Mac."

Russo gripped the tiller to keep Dog on a steady heading. They were halfway to the beach now. Another tank disappeared.

"We're going to make it," he said. "And then you can all salute my ass."

But they were drifting. The strong cross current steadily pushed them east. They weren't going to land on the Dog Red landing zone and would be lucky to make it to Easy Red.

Swanson straddled the gun barrel, binoculars aimed forward. "Loads of hedgehogs, but we can get around them. Seawall along the top of the shingle, and after that, sand dunes. We ain't getting through that unless the engineers blow some holes. I see some beach villas on the right, and some pillboxes."

"They'll be our first targets," Russo said.

The rumble of big engines made him turn. Half the DDs had vanished. Landing craft plowed the sea around him, stirring up waves that lapped over the freeboard and made him clench the grab bar.

The Destroyers had already lost half their strength and were late to boot. The infantry was going to beat them to the beach.

Rockets howled in a shrieking chorus through the air in plumed arcs and rippled across the beach and heights. A vast wall of water and sand sprayed into the air. Another salvo followed on the heels of the first, then another and another in an endless barrage.

"I ain't sure they're having any effect," Swanson said. "I got to say, though, they're sure impressive."

"Destroyers 2, this is Destroyers 2 Actual," the radio said. "We're getting way off track. Correct course to starboard."

Russo turned the tiller, angling Dog to the right.

Clay pulled himself halfway out of the driver's hatch. "Don't do it, Shorty!"

"What?"

"You're going to sink us!"

Dog was in trouble. The waves now battered the DD's side and spilled over the freeboard to slosh around Russo's feet.

"Sail *with* the waves," Clay shouted.

"We have our orders, *goombah*!"

"Just do it! Do it now!"

Russo wrenched the tiller. "All right!"

"Destroyers 2, we're abandoning tank," the radio said.

Delilah went down coughing bubbles.

"Dag nab it," Swanson said. "They're *all* going down."

The heavy swell quickly swallowed most of the remaining tanks. Buoyed by lifejackets, heads bobbed on the water. Other DDs were foundering, their frantic crews bailing water with buckets.

Then, one by one, they sank too.

"I don't see anybody," Russo said in rising panic. "Who's there? Who's left?"

Swanson swept the sea with his binoculars. "I see Duck Soup. That's it."

Russo blew a relieved sigh. "And us. We're still floating. Good call, Eugene."

"What are you happy about, Mac?" the loader said. "You know what this means, right?"

"I know it means we aren't drowning."

"It also means every single Kraut on the beach will be shooting at us."

He was right. With only Duck Soup for company, Dog and its stubby, high-shouldered profile would make a highly visible target for the German gunners.

Ahead, the landing craft ground onto the beach or sandbars and dropped their ramps. Columns of GIs struggled out with their heavy equipment. Flashes winked along the bluffs. White geysers shot out of the sea around Dog as mortars ranged in.

"Hail Mary, full of grace," Russo prayed. "Get in the tank, Animal. Gunner, HE, stand by for target."

The loader shucked his life jacket and dropped into the turret. Dog rode the rollers, surrounded by splashes. Shrapnel clattered off the hull from a nearby hit.

"Hail Mary, full of grace!" Russo cried into the wind.

Once vast and threatening, the sea shrank while the land expanded until it filled his view. The sun continued to rise, exposing the coast and its defenses in its dawn glare. He saw the sand slope up toward the shingle, the tall bluffs across the beach flat, pillboxes and beach villas. And the draw, a paved road that would take them off the beach, if only they could reach it.

"Hail Mary!"

The beach ahead erupted in wet sand that rained across Dog in clumps. Shrapnel ripped through the canvas and zinged off the turret.

"Full of grace! This is it! This is it! We're going in!"

Dog struck the beach drawing fire from every gun on the heights.

ABOUT THE AUTHOR

Craig DiLouie is an author of popular thriller, apocalyptic/horror, and sci-fi/fantasy fiction.

In hundreds of reviews, Craig's novels have been praised for their strong characters, action, and gritty realism. Each book promises an exciting experience with people you'll care about in a world that feels real.

These works have been nominated for major literary awards such as the Bram Stoker Award and Audie Award, translated into multiple languages, and optioned for film. He is a member of the Horror Writers Association, Science Fiction and Fantasy Writers of America, and International Thriller Writers.

Learn more about Craig's writing at www. CraigDiLouie.com. Sign up for Craig's mailing list to be the first to learn about his new releases.

Other books by Craig:

Crash Dive Series
Our War
One of Us
Suffer the Children
The Retreat Series
The Alchemists
The Infection
The Killing Floor
Tooth and Nail
The Great Planet Robbery